**A SUSPENSE THRILLER BASED ON A TRUE STORY
INTERWOVEN WITH FICTION**

TRACK
DOWN

CAL BYERS AND WENDY BRUNNER

DB Press

Track Down
All Rights Reserved.
Copyright © 2016 Cal Byers and Wendy Brunner
v2.0 r1.1

DB Press

ISBN: 978-0-578-17196-8

PRINTED IN THE UNITED STATES OF AMERICA

Contents

Contents

Foreward

A CALL TO DUTY

THERE'S A WAR going. It's been going on for decades and has been becoming harder to fight every year. It's called the war on drugs. Countries all over the world have taken part in the war, yet never seem to gain an advantage. According to a 2014 report by the Office of National Drug Control Policy, illegal drug users in the United States spend around $100 billion annually on cocaine, heroin, marijuana, and meth. A similar United Nations report puts the figure at $150 billion if North and South America, and the Caribbean are combined. And, globalization that has spurred growth in the business world has also become an integral player in the world of illegal drugs. The same United Nations report puts the total retail sales of illegal drugs at $320 billion globally.

From the numbers, it's not hard to see that the United States is at the center of illegal drug use and the illegal drug trade. There truly is a war going on to stop the ever-increasing flow of drugs, and the accompanying narco-terrorists, from entering the United States. The cartels and drug smugglers line their pockets, while destroying the lives of millions of people, young and old. Most of the drugs entering the United States come from countries like Mexico, some Central American countries, and Columbia and Venezuela in South America. The drugs travel up the land routes in trucks and cars, through international waters on boats, on airplanes and by countless other forms and methods that are always shifting to avoid detection.

The prisons in the U.S. are overflowing with people dealing in illegal drugs, or those caught up in using them, making illegal drugs a big, national problem. The federal, state, and local governments are doing what they can to stop the flow, but the task is overwhelming. The government finds and destroys much of the drugs shipped across the border, but with such a large and endless supply there are still plenty leftover to hit the streets of the United States.

Unfortunately, the kingpins of the illegal drug trade live in countries where there is no extradition policy or where they are protected by the government. In many cases, the U.S has its hands tied. However, for many years a covert operation has been in place; one that is never talked about. A campaign against drugs that seeks no media attention, has no slogan and no political ambitions or clout. The aim of the operation is to go after these drug kingpins directly where they live and operate. This story is about a team of three men who signed on voluntarily for the campaign to do just that. You may call them outside contractors or mercenaries, but these men are loyal and dedicated citizens of the U.S. doing their part to stop this cancer in the world.

Because of politics, the U.S. government is reluctant to use official personnel to eliminate these criminals. This kind of program is nothing new though. For centuries, countries around the world have used private military companies to help address a crisis they neither have the means, nor perhaps the political will, to handle.

The dictionary describes a mercenary as a professional soldier, hired to serve in a foreign army. A mercenary has no stake in the outcome of the conflict. Through the centuries, the term mercenary has gained a negative connotation, hinting at private gain being the only motivation. But, private gain does not always have to be in the form of money.

Today, there are other motivations for foreign volunteers who carry out military-style operations. Their primary motives are varied and personal, so mercenaries are now known as outside contractors.

The men in these stories were chosen because of their past service to the U.S. Military and their law enforcement background. They volunteered to hire on with the government to help stop the drug trade and to fight terrorists. Their motivation was not monetary; the pay they received was secondary. Each one of the men, Don Ballantine, Bob Kiser, and Manny Perez had their own personal history and experience in law enforcement and the military. What they had in common was that they spent their lives in the service of the United States and what it stands for.

One must congratulate the bravery and dedication of these three individuals, and many more like them, and be thankful for their willingness to volunteer for the dangerous missions they were sent on into hostile environments.

Chapter 1
HONDURAS

DON'S EYES POPPED open when he heard the slamming of the screen door. He rolled to his side and tried to focus. He was lying on a hammock made of grass rope, on the porch of a rundown shack, on the outskirts of Tegucigalpa in Honduras. He swatted mosquitos from his face, while shielding the blinding sunrise with his other hand. An empty wine bottle lay on the floor beside him. Every muscle in his body ached from his hangover and, he felt as if his tongue was still asleep. His teeth itched and even his hair hurt.

He rubbed his fingers over his day-old stubble and tried to slap himself awake. Gazing down at his chest, he spotted stains of blood on his white shirt and pants. His feet were bare, and he had no idea where his shoes were. He groaned, trying to recall how he had gotten there. It took him a few minutes before he could think straight, and the events of the previous night began to flash back to him.

Inside the shack he heard the voice of his contact in Honduras, Circero, speaking in Spanish. He peaked through the unscreened window and saw Circero was talking to a beautiful girl. Don remembered her from last night. Her name was Juanita. That much, he remembered.

He snapped awake and it all came rushing back. He had arrived in Honduras from the United States just the day before. The rough landing on the Tegucigalpa airfield had scared the hell out of him. He had never experienced such a landing, even in Vietnam. He could easily see from one end of the runway to the other, which didn't seem long enough to land a jet. On top of that, it was constructed on the side of a mountain. He knew the pilot either had to land that plane perfectly and brake fast, or risk falling off the 160 foot cliff. Don was more than happy when the wheels hit solid ground and he could get off the plane. But, he was already worrying about what takeoff would look like.

The airport was a typical South American jumble of chaos; loud shouting in rapid Spanish, people wandering about looking lost, luggage held together with red and white striped nylon rope and piled, to the point of toppling, onto a rickety luggage cart. He could hear an occasional chicken squawk as he waited in line for his bag. He had no problem clearing the usual customs and immigration checkpoints. They didn't ask questions and he just kept his mouth shut. Winding through the maze of people, he took in his surroundings, the location of the gates, the exits, the entrances, just in case. Finally, he walked outside into the humid South American air. Immediately, a beater blue Chevy pulled up to the curb where he was standing.

"Are you Don?" the heavily accented voice inside the car called out.

"That's me. And who are you?" Don answered.

"They call me Circero. We will be working together. Please. Get into the car."

Circero reached across the seat and opened the door from the inside. Don kept his bag with him and slipped into the passenger's seat. Once inside the car, Don kept up the conversation with his new contact. He took a good look at him a few times, acted at ease, yet all the while he was sizing this guy up. When he was on a mission Don never trusted anyone he didn't already know, no matter where he was. That was just smart business. If he was going to work with this guy, he had to make sure he felt confident and comfortable with his new dark-skinned Spanish partner.

As Circero sped away from the airport, he began immediately explaining what role he would play in helping Don to eliminate the target: a prick named Rafael Medina. Don had already been briefed back in Arizona, but he listened attentively to make sure what he already knew, and what this guy was saying, were the same thing. There was no room for error or miscommunication. Lives were on the line, including his own.

They discussed Rafael Medina and both agreed he was a real piece of shit. He was a lieutenant in the dangerous Pacific Cartel and had dealings in every crime imaginable, including smuggling of hundreds of tons of cocaine and heroin into the United States. To support his operation, Medina ran gunrunning and even dealt in human trafficking. Medina was a Lebanese national and a cold-blooded killer. He supported a militia group of thugs hiding out in the mountains surrounding the city. Medina was an ambitious criminal and had aspirations of taking over as head of the cartel operating in Honduras.

But to the poor, Medina was like a God. He resided in a small town named Danlí, just outside of Tegucigalpa. The United States State Department knew Rafael Medina was directly involved in, or had ordered, hundreds of executions, and knew he and his cronies had eliminated judges, lawyers, witnesses, and anyone who might interfere with his quest to become the new Honduran Scarface.

Don started to feel OK about Circero. He could work with this guy. They agreed that what they were about to do was necessary, was the only way to stop this thug who felt shielded from any law or government by his money and power. It was time to put the plan into action.

It was simple really. The plan was to eliminate Medina, showing no trace of who did it or why it was done. Don knew the only thing the U.S. government cared about was that the situation with Medina be handled immediately and quietly.

Circero reached over into the glove compartment of the Chevy and pulled out a 9 mm Beretta with two clips of ammo. Circero assured Don the weapon was sterile. The gun was not traceable and meticulous care had been taken to make it that way. The serial numbers on the frame were ground off by machine, and the pistol had been completely taken apart and cleaned. Everything was removed. Any fibers, hair, or trace evidence including fingerprints were scrupulously cleared. The pistol itself was made in one country and the bullets and clips were made in another country. The Beretta had been wiped clean and loaded by some unknown person somewhere, wearing gloves. Don took out a new handkerchief still in its packaging, carefully wrapped the gun and put it in his coat pocket. He didn't want any fibers from his own clothes getting on this weapon. If the wrong people got a hold of it and found a piece of lint from his coat pocket, someone would be knocking on his door.

Circero had been following Medina for three and a half days before Don arrived so he already had a pretty good idea of his comings and goings.

"Don, this guy takes a walk with his dog every night at about 7 p.m. On his way back, he always cuts through an alley close to his house and goes in his back gate."

This sounded like the perfect place to take Medina down.

"What kind of dog does he have?" Don asked hoping, it would be a little Chihuahua.

"It's a fucking pit bull man."

"Shit. Okay, I'll take care of Medina and you shoot the dog, but only if you have to."

They spent the rest of the afternoon casing the town, looking for vantage points, opportunities and routes of escape. At 5 p.m. they went to Medina's neighborhood. The barrio itself was a jumble of long narrow roads with small shanties lining each side. The shanties were made of corrugated metal and cardboard. Some of the nicer shacks were made of unpainted concrete block. Colorful but dusty curtains stirred in the light breeze and dogs lazed about the front doors, unwilling to stir until the cool of night had come. Around one corner, they came upon an enormous Spanish-style casa behind iron gates and protected by armed guards. Don knew who lived here.

"This is where he lives," Circero said, pointing at the

casa, sticking out like a sore thumb from the surrounding buildings. The guards were lazing against the wall and didn't seem interested in their own surroundings.

"Business must be good for this cocksucker," Don said sarcastically.

"Si, his hands are in everything around here."

They drove around the neighborhood looking for a good place to park where they wouldn't stand out and that had easy access to the alleyway.

"Medina thinks he is indestructible. He has no fear of the people here. When he goes out for a walk, he greets everyone with a big smile. He has no worries. He has a string of whorehouses in the area too, some close to his home. Some days he visits those and when he comes home he goes through that alley there."

Circero pointed to an alleyway. The shadows were growing longer with the setting sun. He parked the car out of site and they waited for dark.

Don thought about how this asshole walked around alone, unafraid, and secure in his feeling of power, greatness and entitlement. We'll see how great he is after we get down to business, he thought.

"Is he always armed?" Don asked.

"Oh yes."

After surveying the alley, Don decided he would position himself behind a fire escape, and Circero would position himself behind a nearby dumpster. Each knew what had to be done and that it had to be done quickly. They slipped into position without being seen. They waited. As darkness approached, Don had flashbacks of Vietnam. He once again felt like he had before a battle. His heart was beating faster, his palms were sweaty, and he had a distinct sense of the fear that had always served him well when placed in a life and death situation.

Suddenly, they both heard the footsteps of their target coming closer. Don knew the first part of his fear would soon be over, and the second wave would kick in. When the actual combat began, or in this case, the killing of another human being, he would be working on pure adrenalin. His focus on the task at hand would be like a laser beam. His muscles would respond with hair trigger precision, allowing him to do quickly and efficiently what had to be done. As Medina approached, Don silently reached down and pulled his knife out of his boot. He clutched the knife tightly, because he knew he would have only one chance to attack before the target would pull a gun on him.

Across the alley, Circero made a sharp noise that quickly got the attention of Medina. Medina looked towards the other side of the alley away from Don, and Don quickly made his move. He jumped out of the darkness from behind Medina, raised the blade, and made perfect contact between Medina's shoulder blade and neck. He drove the knife deeper and on an angle into his throat, making sure to cut the carotid artery and ensure death. Medina fell to his knees and grabbed his throat with both of his hands as he hit the ground. Gasping for air and holding his neck, Medina tried to look at the men, but it was too late. The blood gurgled and filled his throat, and in the last few seconds of his life the blood leached out of his body into a large pool on the dirty ground, and it was over.

Thankfully, with all the commotion the pit bull ran down the alley and out of sight. Some attack dog, Don thought. But, it's always been easier to kill a man than hurt an animal. Men often deserve it, animals don't.

Circero and Don quickly searched Medina's body and removed his watch, ring, wallet, money, belt, and shoes. They quickly put them into a trash bag that Circero would dispose of later. Casually and calmly, they both walked out of the alleyway and to the car. They left the area immediately, and as far as anyone would ever know, Medina was just another victim of a street robbery. They drove back to the shack where they had to wait for a plane the next day to take Don back to the States.

Once they arrived back to the shack, the third wave took over, just as Don expected. Just like in Vietnam. His sweaty palms, the nervousness and his rapidly beating heart, the scared feeling before the battle; these had served him well. The action part, as the attack began was fast and furious, and thrusting the knife into Medina was intense. There was no time to think about being scared.

But now the third wave—after the battle or assault— was taking over. Once he had a chance to sit back and relax, he began to think about what he had been through. His throat became extremely dry and he felt like he could drink ten gallons of water. His hands began to tremble. He was coming down.

Circero handed Don a bottle of wine and a glass. Don smiled and laughed. It was just what he needed.

"Is this the only bottle we have here?" He was testing, hoping for the right answer.

Circero grinned and laughed as he opened a cupboard where there were five more bottles sitting unopened. Don lifted his glass of wine in Circero's direction.

"I couldn't have done it without you."

And with that toast, Don began the long night of trying to forget.

Now, the morning after, lying on the hammock struggling to awaken, Don tried to think of the beautiful Juanita. He sure hoped they had had fun last night. He couldn't remember.

He was ready to get out of this place. He went inside.

"Hey. Buenos Dias man." Cicero greeted him with a big wide grin. He must not have drunk as much as Don had last night.

Juanita just smiled.

"Good morning," was all Don offered in return.

There wasn't too much to say. The deed was done, and neither he nor Circero really wanted to talk about it any further. He went behind the curtain that served as privacy for the bathroom, washed up a little, and changed his shirt. After all, he didn't want to look like a man who had just taken out a major player in the world's largest and most ruthless drug cartel.

Circero drove him back to the airport, this time in a gray beater Ford. The blue Chevy was likely long gone, along with Medina's personal effects, the knife and the Beretta, even though they hadn't been used. Don knew these guys were good at getting rid of things so there would be no questions later. At least he hoped so. It was out of his control though. He had to trust the in-country help set up by the men behind the scenes.

They finally took off for the airport and Circero stopped the car at the departures door. The men shook hands across the seat.

"Good luck and thanks," said Circero.

"Thanks for the assist. It was a good job," Don replied.

"Yeah, no problem. Maybe we'll meet and do it again someday."

"Yeah, sure," Don chuckled. "Good luck to you."

But they both knew, in their hearts, they would never see each other again. This was how it worked. You met. You did your job together. You said goodbye. No ties. No reminiscing over a bottle of wine someday. No future. You shared an intense experience with someone, but when it was over, it was yours and yours alone.

Don opened the car door and walked into the airport, struck immediately by the noise and the smell of jet fuel. His flight left in thirty minutes. He wished it was five. First he had to face the white-knuckle departure from this extreme airfield. But that was nothing compared to facing the next few hours alone on a plane, wrestling with his thoughts about what he had just done.

Chapter 2
HOME

DON'S PLANE LANDED in Phoenix just as the sun was setting. The desert landscape, though stark and dry, actually looked beautiful in the fading light. The last rays of the day lit up South Mountain in shades of red, orange, and pink. The shadows of the giant saguaro cactus stretched out long over the creosote and brittlebushes. Honduras was just a memory now. It had to be that way. He had taken just the last few hours to process the previous forty-eight, and to find an uneasy peace in his own mind. When he got off the plane he would flip the switch and become Don from Mesa again; an ex-cop who had left the cold winters of Chicago to retire quietly in the desert. When he pulled in his driveway, he would settle back into his normal life at home.

"How was your trip?" Diana, his wife, asked when he came through the door.

"Business as usual. Con Air needed a forced deportation for a hundred Hondurans," he lied.

That was part of his cover. Diana, and everyone else he knew, thought he was an air marshal working for the Justice

Prisoner and Alien Transportation System (JPATS), nicknamed "Con Air". They had a hub in Mesa and marshals were usually former military and police guys who had been trained and hired to transport convicts to prisons, and illegals out of the country. Don felt bad for lying, but at least the Honduran part was true.

Don set his bag down in the tiled foyer and headed for the wet bar in the corner of the comfortable, high-ceilinged living room. A nice glass of wine was one way to keep his thoughts from racing and to keep him from discussing any of it with Diana.

"Oh honey, we're supposed to play pinochle at the Mortenson's tonight."

Her voice flowed cheerily through the open space from the kitchen.

Don was glad. A harmless game of pinochle with friends would be a good distraction and help take his mind off his thoughts. By now he'd learned that keeping busy was the best way to control his emotions. A couple of glasses of wine before dinner, a little unwinding at home, and he would be ready to become the life of the party at the Mortenson's.

Pouring himself a glass of wine, he looked in the bar mirror. He didn't like what he was looking at. He knew this mission had taken a toll on him mentally and physically. He could feel it. Maybe he was getting too old. He carried the bottle of wine and moved out to the back patio where he settled in a comfortable lounge chair. He stared out into oblivion for half an hour, enjoying the sounds of the desert settling down for the night and Diana moving about in the kitchen. The wine was kicking in, and it started to help his dark mood a bit. Part of him wished he didn't need the alcohol to feel better, but there were worse things he could be doing. He knew it would help if he could talk to someone about what he had done the night before, but that's not how these things went. Sometimes he worked with other team members, and only the other members of the squad and his in-country contacts ever knew what was going on. Even then, no one ever knew the whole story. Everyone disappeared after the mission was accomplished, so, Don kept it all locked up inside, trying to lead a normal life. He was under strict orders not to discuss his missions with anyone, especially his family members. He loved Diana, she was his best friend, but he couldn't say a word to her and it ate him up inside.

He was leading a double life, and sitting there in the approaching darkness, trying to decompress, the doubts began to creep into his thoughts. He wondered how long he could continue the cover up with the ones he loved.

His life had been filled with violence and killing. While in the Army, he had killed the enemy in Vietnam. Then, he had served on a police department in the northwest suburbs of Chicago for twenty-seven years, and he had seen the worst kinds of criminals imaginable. And now, he was a member of a squad whose sole purpose was to use violence to ensure individuals posing a threat to the United States were defeated. His entire life had been dedicated to the service of his God and country, but at his age maybe he was just getting tired of the pressure. It was wearing hard on him. Of course, he felt honored to serve on this three-man outside contractor unit, but why had they asked him, he wondered. He was beginning to doubt his ability to carry out some of the missions they gave him and then to live with the consequences. Living with the consequences, unable to talk to anyone, was taking a toll on his personal life. Maybe it was time to end it all.

But, he had learned one big life lesson through it all. He had learned the hard way how experiencing these difficult situations of death and violence and danger secretly took away what you loved. It had happened when he returned from Vietnam, and now he felt it could happen again. When he came home from serving in the war, after getting blown up in the hills above the Kim Song Valley, he brought a lot more back with him than he had left with. At the time, he couldn't see it for himself. Back then, with a wife and baby to take care of, he had hoped that the military was going to be his savior, but it ended up destroying everything he loved. It took him the loss of his first marriage and twenty years to see that he had come back with a violent temper and a huge, though well-hidden, drinking problem.

Maybe today it's different, he thought. Maybe today the stigma of seeking psych help is gone. But in those days, if you admitted you were having trouble dealing with what happened to you and your buddies over there, you'd never get a job. He'd stayed in the Army even after they'd offered him a medical discharge, because back then, if you didn't have a clean DD-214, your future was pretty dim. He always felt a deep sense of duty to his family and to his country, and that served him well in the military. When he returned home, he still felt strongly that he had to take good care of his young family. He had to provide a good income, and though the Army had ruined him, he knew he could still salvage something for his family using his military benefits. The choices he made at the time were all for his family, not for himself personally. Sure, he was driven in his career, but what drove him was not personal gain or ego, it was a sense of duty and responsibility. He supposed that's what kept him sane after the war when a lot of guys ended up with serious mental issues. He knew he was strong and driven, but others couldn't handle the feelings they were left with either because of the things they had had to do over there, or because of the long periods of thinking you could die at any moment, or worse, be captured, and tortured.

A pack of coyotes took up howling in the nearby wash and startled Don out of his increasingly dark thoughts. The sound of coyotes howling in the night could send chills up your spine. The high-pitched yipping and yelping of the pack sounded like babies crying and screaming. He knew something had gotten eaten out there in the night and it made him a little sad, though he knew it was only nature.

Slowly, over the next couple of weeks, life got back to normal for Don. His retirement from the police department had given him a good pension and he lived in a nice home with his third wife, Diana. It turned out that Diana, not the army, had been his savior. After his first wife had left him, because she grew up and he never did, he went through a rough time and ended up in lousy second marriage with the wrong woman. Owning up to that wasn't easy, but he knew he had to make some changes if he was going to move forward. So, he let the second wife have everything and he started over once again.

By this time he was a lieutenant in the police department.

He had a good income, good friends, and as the second divorce came through he felt like he was finally ready to get things together. Diana had been his secretary at the department. She was going through a divorce also and she and Don found they could relate to each other on many levels. It was nice and easy. They started out as friends, going out to dinner, sharing stories and the problems they had while trying to navigate their way to new lives. Though Diana was twenty years younger, they really had a lot in common. She understood him, accepted him, and made him happy. He supposed in many ways he was a different guy than he was in his other marriages. It had taken both of them a while to get over their fear of starting something new and having it fail. Once they realized they loved each other and they were both free, they left the cold Chicago winters for sunny Arizona and never looked back.

So here he was in Mesa, living the good life. He was retired and Diana was working at the police department. He and Diana had a great relationship. They were both slow about rushing into a marriage, especially after the big move and complete change in both their lives. But, finally it was clear that it was time to dive into marriage again. Don wanted to give Diana whatever she wanted. He was still a dedicated and devoted man. So, he told her to choose wherever she wanted for the wedding. What woman wouldn't choose a beach in Jamaica? It was a small wedding, just a few friends, but the party was great.

The party part of life was easy. To all his friends Don was always the one in a good mood, always the one smiling. He enjoyed making people laugh and always had a joke on the tip of his tongue. Maybe he used humor to hide what was going on inside, but to him it was better than sulking in a corner all the time. Don and Diana socialized at cookouts, pool parties, and went out dancing often. No one ever suspected he was living this double life. He even found work at the Dobson Ranch Golf Course in Mesa. It was a good cover and something to get him out of the house.

But after a mission, during the time of trying to adjust to his regular life, he often asked himself why he was doing this. In his mind he was convinced he was doing his patriotic duty. The scumbags he was eliminating deserved their fate. As far as he was concerned these guys were just taking up good people's air. There was no real loss when they left this earth. He was, in no way, mourning the loss of their human life, but he did wonder sometimes, was he just killing to kill? Was he just in it for the adrenalin rush?

Beyond thinking about the actual mission, there was another source of anxiety for Don. Every day held an uncertainty. Every day there was the anticipation, and not the good kind people feel when they know something new and exciting is going to happen. This was anticipation that came with anxiety. The kind that comes when you are expecting, and just waiting, for something stressful to happen again, for the other shoe to drop. When would the phone ring again? How much longer before being asked to travel to some strange place again? Will the next knock at the door be some authorities from a government agency wanting to know what he has done, who was with him and who he worked for? Of course, if that happened, would the people he works for really protect him or just throw his unit under the bus, denying knowledge of the team and completely isolating them to fend for themselves? That was one of the problems. It had been a problem in Vietnam. It had been a problem on the police force every time they got a call. Maybe he was getting tired of this feeling. The fear of the unknown, and what was coming next, constantly gnawed at him.

Chapter 3
CHICAGO

DON LIKED TO keep in shape and he worked out at a local gym once a week. Not only was he trying to burn off extra energy, he felt he had to keep his body fit to accomplish the grueling missions. On his three-mile jogs he could clear his mind while working off some belly fat. On one occasion he was a mile into the run and found himself thinking about the work. He wondered: Why in the hell do I take these dangerous government assignments at my age? He thought it must be true; he must be an adrenaline junkie. He couldn't help but smile. He was feeling good so he didn't care how he got his rush. After all, he wasn't hurting anyone who didn't deserve it.

As his mind wandered, it got him thinking about his first meeting with the mysterious man named Peter, who never divulged exactly what government agency he worked for, or anything else about himself. Don suspected he was with the State Department or maybe the CIA. Peter knew everything about Don. He had his complete service records from Vietnam, everything about his police force career, as well as his training at the FBI National Academy. Peter was well aware of Don's outstanding record of dedication, heroics and courage wherever he served. He also knew Don had no outward fear of any situation or any person. That's how Don had to be to survive in Vietnam and on the police force. Patrol cops never know what to expect when they arrive on the scene. There could be crazy people, weapons, or sometimes, crazy people with weapons. Whatever the situation, as a cop he had to deal with it and survive, and that's exactly what he did for over twenty-seven years.

There were plenty of times when he felt he was in danger while on the police force. But one incident he'd rather have forgotten about always remained fresh on his mind, mostly because it almost ended his career and called his integrity into question. It was the day he and his partner were called out on a domestic incident at a three-story rundown apartment complex on the north side of the city. They'd both had their share of handling domestic calls before, but this call was different. As a cop you just never know which call is going to be the one that will change your life forever.

The building was in a rough area of the city to begin with so Don and his partner were on edge going in. As they came up to the door of the apartment in question, they could hear a women screaming. They knocked on the door forcefully and heard the woman scream again followed by loud crashing sounds, as if stuff was being thrown around. Without hesitating any longer, Don threw his weight against the door, busting the frame and sending wood splinters flying.

They burst into the room shouting, "Police officers! Police! Don't move! What's going on here?" Both he and his partner made sure it was clear that the law had arrived.

They hadn't moved from the doorway and were surveying the situation before making another move. Their guns were pointed across the small room at a giant of a man with his shirt off and a surprised look on his face. He must have been over 6' 10" and weighed over three hundred and fifty pounds. He froze when the door had been broken in, and now the giant was glaring at both of them. Don could tell he didn't like this sudden intrusion into his home, and as Don looked more closely the man definitely seemed to be drunk or on drugs. There didn't appear to be a weapon, and it didn't look like this guy could move quickly to grab one either. He was swaying a little bit and looked like he was trying to focus and figure out exactly who was standing in front of him.

It was quiet for a moment. Then a loud voice came from the door down the hall.

"He's going to kill me," the woman screamed. Don figured she was this guy's wife or girlfriend.

"Shut the fuck up," the giant hissed as he picked up a lamp from the nearby end table and threw it against the closed bedroom door, sending glass flying across the room.

"OK. OK," Don said calmly, not moving from the door. "Let's just calm down and we can figure this out."

But that didn't help, and the guy started hurling whatever he could get his hands on at the bedroom door; an ashtray, a magazine, a glass of something, a couple of beer bottles. Don tried to get him to calm down again, but he wasn't having any of it and continued his rampage.

Don moved slowly closer, talking calmly to the giant. "Sir, just calm down and we can get this all figured out. Let's not get anyone hurt."

"Fuck that," he spat as he hurled a tchotchke down the hall, the Windy City memento gouging a hole into the cheap wood door.

"I'm sick of her shit. I'm sick of all of you." He reached under the chair cushion and immediately Don and his partner knew they had no choice. They had to take him down physically and cuff him to calm him down.

Before he could pull out whatever was under the cushion, they were on him. The giant threw a punch at Don and the brawl began. For five straight minutes they fought this guy. He was big and strong and he wrestled and punched like a wild animal. It was two on one, but their combined weight was almost no match for this behemoth. The giant would not give up. Finally, his size got the better of him as he began sweating profusely and Don and his partner saw he was getting tired. Just as they had him in a position to cuff him, he dropped to the floor and Don saw his eyes roll into back in his head. His huge body convulsed for a few moments then became still. It was apparent that he was unconscious.

"What the hell happened to him?" Don's partner asked, gasping for air.

Don checked the guy's vitals. "Damn, this guy's not breathing. Quick, call the paramedics. We gotta get a supervisor over here." His partner radioed the paramedics.

Don rechecked the man's vitals. "Damn. The medics aren't gonna help this guy. He's dead."

Sensing the quiet, the woman came out of the bedroom

and immediately began screaming when she saw the giant on the floor.

"Oh my god! What have you done to him? What did you do?"

One of her eyes was black and she had a nosebleed. She fell on his chest crying and moaning. It was as if she had lost the love of her life when only minutes before she claimed he was trying to kill her. Don and his partner just stood there. There was nothing else they could do except wait for the paramedics and the supervisor.

After that, Don and his partner were put on a paid administrative leave until internal affairs could investigate. In the meantime, the wife filed a multimillion-dollar lawsuit against both the officers and the police department. She claimed they killed her husband on purpose with excessive force: police brutality. The case was highly publicized in Illinois and eventually she took it all the way to the Illinois Supreme Court.

During the long wait while the case made its way through the legal system, Don was in limbo. His fate was uncertain. Was he going to lose the job he had devoted his life to because of some asshole drunk wife-beater? After months and months of agonizing waiting, Don fell into a depression again. He started drinking every night at the local bar, La Margarita. It was a police bar downtown. All the Cook County sheriffs hung out there. It's where the guys went after their shift to unwind and trade stories. Sometimes they even solved some crimes over a game of pool in the back.

One night, early in his career he went to the bar after a shift, Don was playing a casual game and talking to a buddy who asked, "What'd you do tonight?"

"Home invasion and attempted sexual assault on a 14-year-old girl," Don was still hurting over the sight of that scared little innocent girl.

"Whaddya have? What's he look like?"

"Not much. The girl can ID him. Witness saw a white wide-track, maybe a Trans Am. I found a lens from his glasses on the floor. That little girl must have fought him pretty good. Right lens. That's about all I've got."

Don's buddy, who was ready to take a shot, stood up, the tip of his stick tapped on the tile floor and he stared straight at Don.

"No shit Don. Tonight I arrested this guy. His name was Jesse James, no lie. But, fuck if he didn't have glasses with the right lens missing."

That's how it went sometimes. If you got lucky.

It turned out the guy was locked up in the McHenry County jail already. That brave little girl ID'd him in a lineup and there were plenty of others willing to do the same. He went away for twenty years, no parole. So, the moral of the story for Don was that the drinking wasn't all bad.

La Margarita was a second home for a lot of them. It was a place where they could talk freely about the hell they experienced almost every night in the city. The owner had even given them the keys to lock up when they were done. It was a safe place. A haven.

When he was first put on leave he tried to resist going out, but it was an easy habit to slip into.

A buddy would call in the afternoon. "Don, come have a drink."

"No, can't do it tonight," he'd start out with.

"C'mon Don," the convincing would begin.

"One and done."

"Two and through."

"Three and flee."

He'd chuckle and give in. "OK. OK. Just for a bit."

Before he knew it, it was every night.

He would come home late at night and pass out on the sofa, which was stressing his home life. And though Linda loved Don very much and tried to maintain a home for their family, Don's future was not clear and it was a difficult time. Looking back, Don could see he was a total wreck during this time.

Finally, after months of agonizing about their future, the Supreme Court found the two officers not guilty of any wrongdoing. In fact, the autopsy showed the giant had had a heart attack during the struggle with the officers. Turns out he had a long history of heart disease. Both Don and his partner were reinstated to duty.

Don kept jogging through the park, recalling this incident as though it happened yesterday. He began to tire, and returned home at a slower pace and then slowed to a walk. At his driveway he stopped at the mailbox. Inside was the familiar plain white envelope addressed to him. He opened it and pulled out a receipt. It was printed with the United States Department of Agriculture seal. It showed the department had deposited $10,000 into his bank account. He knew this was his "farmer's" incentive for not growing a certain crop. To the Department of Agriculture, he was just another farmer pocketing his subsidy. That's the way Don got paid by the government for his services. He thought back for a minute to Honduras and to Rafael Medina, whom he had sent to hell, and smiled at the silly way the whole thing was covered up. Him, a farmer. That was funny.

It was a sunny day and Don had to head over to the Dobson Ranch Golf Course to work. As he arrived his supervisor came up and told him attendance had been down. He had some other things to say about complaints of slow play at the golf course and other minor shit. After what Don had been through in Honduras, he had a hard time focusing on the supervisor's complaints. He knew he had to, but he couldn't really take his boss's statements seriously.

These kinds of problems, slow play on a golf course, were trivial to Don, but he knew he needed the job not only as a cover up but to keep himself busy too. Don was good at keeping things hidden, so he simply looked at his boss very seriously and said, "Sure Boss. I'll figure out the problem and get it straightened out. No more complaints."

If there's one thing Don had learned, it was that the job at hand is the most important. And no matter how Don felt about his double life, at this time, the customer's needs at the Dobson Ranch Golf Course were the job at hand.

Chapter 4
CARTELS

IT WAS PRETTY quiet for a while which helped Don's doubts subside. Fading memories were a blessing really. He liked to keep busy, so he used his spare time to study the inner workings of the drug cartels and how they operated around the world. He found it interesting, and besides, he didn't like surprises. He liked to be well prepared, and most of all he wanted to understand the enemy.

To find out more about the cartels, he contacted some of the friends he'd made at the FBI. He started asking a few questions on the subject, but only to people he knew wouldn't think too much about it or try to connect any dots. The world of international drug crime is a treacherous place, so of course, no one would openly talk about or reveal any current working cases to him, at least not overtly. But he learned enough, and knew enough from previous missions, to put some pieces together and figure out how to dig deeper into the world of these criminals.

For him, it was important to "know the enemy." That's why, in Vietnam, they had rummaged around in the North

Vietnamese abandoned camps and backpacks. The best defense was knowing who you were dealing with and what they might do. As far as he was concerned, these cartels poured their poisons through the veins of the nation, especially its young people. With their steady flow of drugs, the cartels had destroyed countless families, ruined good people, and robbed the nation of billions of dollars in health, legal and prison costs, not to mention what they did to people in their own countries. And it never ceased. The river of drugs kept flowing. Some people looked other places for the enemy, the Middle East or Russia, but to Don the enemy was drugs and those who dealt in drugs. If he was going to continue to pull off the dangerous missions his government sent him on, he felt he needed to know more. He didn't want to play defense with these guys. That was a losing game. Just like the mob in places like Chicago, he knew these groups were ruthless and had very long memories. He wanted to know the players and the plays they might make so he could be on the offense.

Thank God for the Internet. A few nights of surfing and he had a pretty good education on the cartels of Mexico, Central America, and South America. These weren't secret organizations either. Some cartels were mentioned directly by name like the Los Zetas, Sinaloa Cartel, Juarez Cartel and the Gulf Coast Cartel; they were proud, they weren't hiding. These powerful and very violent crime syndicates all had the same mode of operation involving drug smuggling, prostitution, gambling, human trafficking, and of course murder. They had even recently become involved in the sale of human organs. Power and money was always their goal and they achieved that goal at any cost.

In Colombia it was coca that meant money. Peasants grew coca for the cartels because of the money, or because they were threatened. Even though their cut was miniscule, it still paid more than food crops. And, the cartels were masters of manipulating local farmers to grow the crop on a massive scale. The biggest and most well-known cartels, based in the cities of Medellin and Cali in Western Colombia, promoted the sowing of coca and it was estimated at one point there were over four hundred thousand acres of coca growing in Colombia. This was eighty percent of the world's supply.

The head of the Medellin Cartel was a guy named Pablo Escobar. The leaders of the Medellin Cartel were flashy; driving fancy cars, buying mansions and just about anything else they wanted, anytime they wanted. The government knew Escobar was responsible for the murder of hundreds of people including judges, lawyers, police, journalists who got too nosey and ordinary citizens who didn't comply with the cartel's demands. But, whether out of fear of retaliation or because the government was in on the money—probably both—they weren't doing much to stop him. The leaders of the Cali Cartel on the other hand were more sophisticated and business astute, but still ruthless. They were the first to start using technology as a tool of the trade. They studied the U.S. government, and the DEA and its moves, in order to stay one step ahead of the government. They began to hire top engineers to design sophisticated communications equipment that could evade bugging by the U.S. They even went so far as to hire Russian engineers to build a submarine, which they were going to use to smuggle cocaine into the U.S. They hired internationally trained heavy-duty lawyers to shield them from laws around the globe. Both groups used terrorist techniques to intimidate their workers, as well as government officials who tried to get in their way. The two groups were warring incessantly and brutally. The only good news was that, along with Mexico, the U.S. was slowly making Colombia and these criminal enterprises ground zero for its war on drugs.

Don read about one incident in Mexico that was not only frustrating, but made him even more determined to do whatever he could to wipe these guys from the earth. These local stories rarely made the world news and were always a bit murky, though the gist was clear. The victims were so afraid of retaliation that they just didn't want to talk. The police and town officials were all on the take. Everyone was covering or protecting something or someone, and the result was that the truth was hard to come by. But, the story went like this. A group of local students was raising money for a trip to Mexico City. They were in a rural area in the south of Mexico and in those poor areas it wasn't uncommon for kids to take to the streets to raise money for a cause. The students wanted to be in Mexico City to protest, and commemorate, the killing of another group of students years before, likely at the hands of the cartel. No justice was ever served from the government, and the lost kids were as good as forgotten by everyone, except for their friends and families. It wasn't right, and every year protests sprang up on the anniversary of their disappearance, yet still nothing had been done to find out what really happened. The government kept stalling and making excuses about why there was no progress in the investigation, and every year the issue became front page for one day, and every year it faded away the next. To raise the money to go to Mexico City, these young activist students canvassed the pueblo asking for donations at intersections and outside of shops and restaurants. As the story goes, when their activities inconvenienced the wife of the town's mayor she called her husband and demanded he get rid of them. He in turn called the police chief and the students were rounded up, never to be heard from again. The townspeople organized searches and demanded investigations, but the local officials and police couldn't seem to find any clue as to how dozens of local young people simply disappeared. Weeks later, a mass burial site was found far outside of town and there were vague confessions by local thugs about murder and shallow graves.

The people of the town knew from years of this kind of thing, that drugs, money, and guns were at the heart of what had happened. They even knew the likely players. The mayor and the police were no doubt in partnership with the local drug lords, and they all worked together to put down any signs of dissent among the people. This infuriated Don. He felt for the poor innocent families who were victimized and for the all the young people who were trying to make a difference. But, the worst part was that these cartels were able to terrorize the people because of their lucrative drug smuggling operations, supplying drugs to the United States. His country was responsible, in part.

As the cartels continued destroying lives around the world, Don felt, as others did, the enemy must be stopped. He knew this cancer could grow beyond the border and the United States could easily be prey to incidents like these if something wasn't done. There were already reports of unexplained disappearances down along the border. He heard a lot more now that he was living in Arizona. When he started reading these kinds of things, his doubts about the missions disappeared, and he was again committed to assisting in any way he could to curb the flow of drugs into the country. But he was not a vigilante. And even though he was technically on his own, he felt the sense of pride and duty he needed to feel by working under the name of the United States of America, even if it was a secret.

Don realized he could never stop man's inhumane treatment of other human beings, but at least he could stop a few of the bastards who were profiting from the deaths of others. For him, the hardest thing about eliminating some of these criminals was not being able to go public and tell the world that one more scumbag had been removed from it. After each mission he wished he could celebrate with the families of the innocent victims and give them a sense that justice had been served.

There's no doubt Don was proud of his work, but there was a dark side. His family life suffered because he had to hide behind these lies and deceptions. His go-to cure was the bottle when the subject of his work came up. It was hard to believe, but his own family didn't know about the dangerous second life he led. He supposed he was a pretty good liar. But, really what he had done was somehow separate the two lives from each other. When he was on a mission, he didn't think of back home. He was focused. He was Don the Outside Contractor, doing a job. And while he had recently begun to have doubts about whether he could do it anymore, he had always been able to put the other Don away. Once he got home and decompressed, he pretty easily became Don the Retired Cop from Mesa. It was hard to explain, almost like a split personality.

On the home front he appeared to lead a normal life. He appeared to be caring to those around him, but at times even that was stressful. He felt there was a light side and a dark side to his personality. His dark side was his government work, and he was good at it. His light side was his personal life, which was much more difficult. Sure, he was always joking around and laughing, behaving like the life of the party, but inside he was hurting. He always had a sense of anxiety and he had yet to learn how to conquer it. He often thought of the 1963 song by Bobby Goldsboro, *See the Funny Little Clown*:

> "No one knows he's crying
> No one knows he's dying on the inside
> 'Cause he's laughing on the outside"

He felt that way. No one really knew what was going on inside. The thing was, he could eliminate a criminal easily, but it was much harder for him to show love or say "I love you" even to his own wife or sons. After all these years, he was beginning to think it was time to change his ways. But that was sure a lot easier said than done.

Nearly his whole life, as far back as he could remember, he had simply been trying to make things right. He had never wanted more than for everyone to be taken care of and to be happy. Maybe he'd missed the small things because he was so busy doing the right thing. Maybe the right thing had actually turned into the wrong thing. It was all so confusing. When you started to look back you could make yourself a little crazy with all the second-guessing.

DON KNEW HE lived with the demons from his past. He also knew exactly when and how it had all started.

Chapter 5
VIETNAM

THE STORY WAS not a new one. Don was a city kid, running the streets, kind of a jerk from the time he was six. When he was twelve, his father died suddenly and his mother worried. So, she sent him to military school for a couple of years. But, by fifteen he was back at home, cutting school and running around with the other kids, looking for something to do. Impressing girls became important, and nothing was beyond the limit. If a girl he liked wanted to go out on a Friday night in a Corvette, he'd just steal one for the night. Putting in some hours working at the corner gas station helped him to buy his own car, a red 1959 Impala white-top convertible. And that car helped him win the girl of his fifteen-year-old dreams. Linda was pregnant by sixteen.

Don may have pushed the limits while he had his fun, but he knew right from wrong. He knew Linda and the baby were his responsibility and it was a role, maybe the first one, that he took seriously. Besides, he loved Linda and he would never turn his back on his child. So, in 1964 at seventeen, and with few other options, he talked his mother into signing the form, went down to the recruiter, and joined the army.

Despite the war, Don had great hopes in what the army could do for him and his young family. It seemed the best way to go. By joining, he'd have steady money and health insurance. The plan was, after basic training he'd give Linda and his baby a name. The army was even going to train him, send him to school, and he wouldn't have to pay for it. There were plenty of good reasons to sign up voluntarily. He could see the future of his family and the army was going to make it happen.

After basic he would bring Linda and the baby with him to his post. He'd work. He'd have insurance. He'd take care of them. It was all going to work out just fine. It felt good to be taking care of important things; that was the plan at least. Instead, the army sent him to Germany. With no marriage certificate, Linda couldn't go. Already, Don was feeling like he got screwed. He was regrouping, figuring out how to get home to Linda, get married, and provide for her and the baby. So, when the call went out for volunteers to head to Vietnam, he signed right up. After all, they were giving pretty good extra combat pay, which would help Linda, plus he'd get thirty days leave to go home, visit with his baby, and get married. That was a lot more than they were offering for him to stay in Germany. The new plan was to do his tour in Vietnam and then come home with good training and a good job in the military, so he and Linda could get on with raising a family. He got back stateside and he and Linda had a small wedding.

Don had turned eighteen in 1965, and a few months

later, with Linda taken care of with money, a name, and surrounded by family, he shipped out. It was a hell of a trip across the Pacific, and right from the start he knew this was something different. Right away, as they were coming into Saigon the enemy was shooting at the plane. Don had never experienced anything like it. The night air was heavy, hot, and steamy. These guys over here—commanding officers, fellow soldiers—most of them were on a different level than Don had seen back in the states or in Germany. The heat, the humid jungle air, and the constant uncertainty hit him hard. Looking back it was a sort of shock. Sure, there was laughter and joking around with each other, but that's what guys did when they were scared as shit and under pressure.

Don found the whole situation confusing from the start. He made it to his unit, tried to regroup and get some bearings about the situation. Who were they supposed to shoot? North Vietnamese, South Vietnamese, Viet Cong, they all looked the same to Don. Charlie was the enemy, but it wasn't clear-cut. Don wasn't in for shooting people at random, it wasn't right. But, when he asked an officer how he could know the difference between the Viet Cong enemy and the South Vietnamese, the answer came quickly,

"You kill'em all and let God sort'em out."

At barely eighteen, Don could only wonder what the hell was going on in this place. After the first three months or so, Don's only focus was on survival. He figured out pretty fast that he could die in Vietnam, and though he didn't care so much about himself, as long as Linda and the baby were taken care of, he was going to learn how to protect himself in this hellhole.

Don was in B Company, 1st Battalion of the 12th Calvary Division. When he first arrived, he figured out pretty quickly that a mistake had been made and that he was the only "leg" in an airborne outfit. Don was going to have to jump out of a CH-47 helicopter, when all he'd ever jumped out of before was bed. The army had neglected to train him for that detail, so the guys took him under their wing and trained him themselves. Don learned PLF, a parachute-landing fall, off a mess hall table. Those guys taught him how to be Army Airborne.

Out of his almost eight months in Vietnam, most of it was spent in the jungle on patrol. He lived in the wild for a month at a time, no showers, no shaving, never even taking off his boots, they'd just move from designated spot to designated spot making sure the enemy was not encroaching on the troops and looking for whatever they could find to get the advantage. Don's nineteenth birthday happened somewhere in the central highlands of Vietnam.

The first few months were hell, just trying to survive and learning what he had to do to see another day—learning how to pretend he wasn't afraid. Guys were just as scared as he was, he knew that, but no one gave in to it. Besides, Don figured the big kids were doing it, so he could do it too. The big kids were only twenty-two.

Night ambush patrol was the toughest. Patrols were made up of four guys and their M-16 rifles with bayonets fixed. They would sleep in two-hour shifts, using one of their watches to keep time. They'd pass it from one guy to the next. But, you never wanted to be that last guy. The last guy always got screwed when the other three shaved a little time off their shift by moving the hands forward a few minutes. The mission was to protect the perimeter and serve as a warning for the company if the enemy was encountered. The rule was: kill anything that entered the perimeter. Anything. There was no way to know who was Charlie and who was not, and that wasn't a call that could be left up to luck. Whoever entered or wandered into the perimeter was the enemy, no questions asked. If the patrol was soft, if they let someone go on their way because they didn't seem harmful, there was a good chance they'd go back and alert Viet Cong fighters who would then ambush the unit in the hot, dark jungle. It had happened plenty of times. So, now the rule was no one was let go. No one was to be trusted. Anyone they saw had to die, by hand if possible, no gunshots. This included the farmer, his wife and ten-year-old daughter. Who knows why they were out there after dark. Maybe they were just getting home late from the fields. Maybe they'd been to town. Maybe they were Viet Cong. Maybe they weren't. Don was sick, but there was no questioning. On word from the leader, the patrol was forced to bayonet them all, not using their guns to keep the rest of the company from leaping into action. He did it, but it had hit Don's mind hard. But, this was what the army had trained Don so well to do. It was over quickly and quietly and not another word was said about the incident in the jungle. At least by Don.

In late December, they were shipped out to heavy fighting and there was plenty of dread in the air. The 12th Calvary had landed directly in the middle of the North Vietnamese Army and took immediate fire. From then on it was constant fighting—three, four nights and days in a row.

He learned later about the supposed Christmas truce and the Bob Hope show at base. But, someone forgot to tell the North Vietnamese Army hiding out in the jungle that there was a truce. They fought right through it. The patrol would come across pockets of Viet Cong and rout them out, going through their supplies and looking for clues to their plans or letters from home with information that could be used against them later, during interrogations.

Don and all the guys were at their limits, trying to be alert to the enemy, follow orders that seemed futile, and deal with the heat, humidity, and bugs of the jungle. Other units were encountering North Vietnamese on every route. On December 29th Don's patrol was hot on the trail of some fighters, sweeping down the side of mountain when they came across the entrance to a cave. Sitting at the entrance was a pile of Vietnamese rucksacks. They started going through them, looking for anything useful. Don moved one of the packs and a leg quickly darted back behind a rock. Don didn't hesitate; he threw a grenade and ran. When he went back to check on the body, it happened. The fighter had survived and threw his own grenade back at Don. It went off right in front of him, hitting his arms, chest, face, legs. It even bent his rifle.

The guys packed him up and he was medevacked out, taking sniper fire in the basket as they hoisted him up to the helicopter. They also took care of the guy who'd thrown the grenade.

After that, he was shipped to Japan for treatment and recovery; three months of operations and hanging around. They finally sent him back to the hospital at Naval Station

Great Lakes where he spent another month. They offered him a medical discharge, but he knew that wasn't going to get him anywhere in life, so he refused it.

Eventually he was released out to Ft. Bliss in El Paso. Linda and the baby joined him and he struggled to put the past eight months behind him. The army set him up as a Non-Commissioned Officer in Charge. His responsibility was running the entertainment on Post. It was a tough job. Basically, he had to sit around and judge the dancers and whether they were showing too much cleavage or too much cheek. The general's and colonel's wives complained if there was too much skin. It was a perfect outlet for Don's personality and for his new problem with the bottle.

In retrospect, those years in the army had been a disaster for Don. When he signed up for service he had had pretty high hopes. The army was going to be his savior. When he went to Vietnam as a young eighteen-year-old he had a smile on his face, was full of hope and determination, and he had no trouble believing the recruitment messages about how he could improve his life with a stint in the army. What he ended up with was severe post-Vietnam stress syndrome. It's not like his problems happened little by little. Bam! He was thrown in, and his life changed. He knew now the experiences over there had haunted him his whole life. It had made him angry inside and unable even to figure out why. It took his first marriage. He now had three sons, and it had affected his relationships with them. God forbid anyone tried to get close to him or fall in love with him. He'd panic and come across as cold and distant, even if he didn't want to be that way. Sure he was nice and kind and helpful, a good guy to have around, but when it came over him, the darkness, there was nothing anyone could do. When he came out of it, all he could do was make amends.

Everyone knew about PTSD now of course, and it gave him some comfort to know he wasn't just crazy or flawed inside. But he had spent a whole life dealing with it on his own. By the time he was twenty-one he had seen too much, his nerves were shot. He got out of the military, joined the police force, and had spent the next couple of decades as a functional alcoholic, trying to control his violent temper. He supposed he was one of the lucky ones, to get away with just a couple of failed marriages and bad relationships. Other guys he knew had really lost it all. Still, he couldn't help but think that if God was a woman, he was screwed.

The PTSD coupled with the stress of his long career on the police force, and now this new career as a paid outside contractor, was beginning to wear on his heart and soul. How much longer could he continue to serve his country and keep his sanity at the same time? More importantly, was it really worth it anymore?

Chapter 6
EL SALVADOR

IT WAS ONE of those hot July days in the Arizona desert with the temperature hitting over one hundred and fifteen degrees. There would surely be monsoon rains in the afternoon. Not many golfers were hardy enough to head out in that kind of heat, so Don came home early. He hit the button on the answering machine, and a familiar tone sent a jolt like lightening through him. He didn't recognize the voice per se, but he knew from the tone, before the words were even spoken, he was getting another call to duty.

The voice instructed him to meet Peter in the bar at the Tempe Mission Palms Resort at 10 a.m. the next day. The voice said he was needed to attend an agricultural training session. He had to chuckle about the cover. He'd never even had a garden in his life, but he knew what it meant: they were preparing for another assignment.

He stood quiet for a moment and with shaking hands deleted the message. He was thinking about the likely possibility of having to go out on an assignment to eliminate someone. After all, they weren't just calling to see how he was. His heartbeat quickened and the adrenaline kicked in. As usual, to calm down, he poured himself a glass of wine. His mind began to race over the possibilities. Where would he be sent to this time? Would he be working alone or with the usual three-man team? Would it be quick and easy or would he have to stay out of the country several days, tracking down the intended target? It sure was going to be a long night and Diana would no doubt comment that he seemed preoccupied. Thankfully, no one was home yet and he let the wine help him process this next adventure. Sleep would be elusive that night.

Don arrived at the Mission Palms Resort at the designated time. Punctuality was important in this business. Being late could mean your life or someone else's. In the bar he spotted Bob Kiser and Manny Perez sitting at a table. The three of them made up the team.

Bob rose to greet him, "Hey, good to see ya buddy," he said, as they heartily shook hands and hugged as old friends do.

Don extended his hand to Manny. "Manny, it's been a while. How ya doin'?"

"Good. Good. No complaints." Manny shook hands and they sat down at the round cocktail table, all pumped up with the good feelings of seeing people you respected and the anticipation of a new mission.

Don and Bob had known each other for a long time. In fact it was Bob who had gotten Don wrapped up in this business to begin with. Don was ambitious in his career and when the opportunity to attend the FBI Academy came to him, he didn't hesitate. The Academy was an elite stop for police officers. Only one fifth of one percent of all the cops in the country were invited to the Academy, and his boss had recommended him personally. He was proud of this and knew it would be a gold star on his resume. Attending the top police school in the country would not only prepare him for new and better opportunities, he knew he would also make top connections, which would serve him for the rest of his life. He was right. He and Bob had gone through the Academy together, and though they were not supposed to discuss anything about their current contract employment situation, they had their own ways of communicating, getting the job done, and remaining good friends.

Bob had gone on to the Secret Service, but they kept in touch after the Academy. Eventually, Don had gone to Arizona and was doing a little work with Con Air out of Williams Gateway airport in Mesa. He still clearly remembered the day, not that long ago, when Bob called him up.

"I got something for us," he said, "Do you want to put your Vietnam skills to work for real good money?"

Don knew it was something interesting. He hadn't known exactly how interesting, or hard, it would become, but it didn't matter at the time. Don just needed something to get the adrenaline pumping again. The sporadic Con Air flights and the golf course weren't cutting it.

The mood changed as soon as they saw Peter enter the bar. The more professional and low-key greetings spoke of the distance always kept between this trio and the man who briefed them.

He didn't sit down, but asked them to come to his room, which they did.

Peter, dressed in his usual black suit and tie, sat behind

a desk and opened his laptop. The jovial atmosphere of the bar was gone. There was a heavy aura of anxiety and anticipation of the unknown hanging in the room. The tension was thick. Don never was one to stay serious for too long, so he broke the tension by cracking a few political jokes. These were the kind of jokes only certain people would understand; inside jokes about politics and law enforcement. These days everything had to be politically correct, and these jokes would certainly never pass that test. Some might even say they were a little sick. But, these guys got it and it cut the tension.

Peter was tapping away at his laptop, preparing what he was going to say. Bob tried his hand at getting Peter to lighten up with a political comment of his own.

"What do we have to do, go down there and find some prostitutes that can keep their mouths shut and not tell everyone about the last time the Secret Service was there to guard the president?"

Everyone laughed. This was a direct shot at the Secret Service, often the brunt of their jokes. Even though everyone in the room had the utmost respect for the Service and the work they did, they all knew the Service had problems. A few bad agents who had no respect for the institution had managed to give a great organization a bad name. It was too bad and Bob, having been an agent, hoped more than most the Service could get it together and get back to the days when guarding the president was the highest honor, and a job treated with reverence.

Peter interrupted the small talk. He directed his attention to all three of them.

"Alright. As you've probably already guessed, this is going to be a three-man operation," he began.

"You will be leaving for El Salvador in two weeks. The person of interest is Jorge "Gongo" Gonzales. He is a known cartel member. He's been deported from the United States four times. He's spent some time in prison here. He is a ruthless, violent individual and not the type you'd invite over for Christmas with your family. The local situation has already been arranged and your contact will meet you at the café in the Rosa Hotel in San Salvador. I have folders here with information on Gonzales and his close contacts. That will get you started for now. I have your flight information here and the final plan will be discussed with your contact after your arrival in San Salvador."

Peter passed around several photos of the target, Jorge "Gongo" Gonzales. No one said much after that, and the meeting broke up. Don drove back to Mesa, and the others went on their way back to wherever they'd come from. There was no further discussion and he knew he wouldn't see them until the plane ride to El Salvador.

In the two weeks prior to leaving for the assignment, Don was in a state of readiness at all times. He was anxious to get it over with. They didn't usually have to wait this long, and he found it hard to stay focused on his ordinary life. The anxiety of not knowing what to expect ate at him every day. He continued his work at the golf course, but the days passed slowly. As with all the assignments he'd been on, he wasn't sure he'd make it back—being killed or captured was a real possibility.

Two weeks later, the three-man team departed Phoenix on schedule, and after a long grueling flight they landed in the capital city of San Salvador. The country was not many years removed from a brutal twelve-year civil war that killed over 75,000 of its people. That was a lot of people for a country smaller than the state of Massachusetts. From the plane it looked like El Salvador was nothing but mountains, but then the plane took a wide turn out over the Pacific to set up a landing on a high plateau at the international airport about twenty miles inland. Don thought about how easy it would be for drug lords to hide out and to move cocaine through those mountains. He understood why it was such a tough battle for the law to get a handle on the drug trade. His type of volunteer warfare was one way to match the tactics of these guys.

The air hung heavy. This was definitely the tropics. The streets of San Salvador bustled with motorcycles and pickup trucks loaded with people hanging off the sides. The buses were crowded too and painted in bright colors and designs, each one making a personal statement about the driver, though looking as if it might not make it to the next corner. They were decorated with religious symbols, flowers, sayings and even fringe with tassels hanging down. The smells were as interesting as the scenery, and the guys just took it all in as they made their way to the hotel in a taxi.

Each of them took a separate room. As always they were checked in as representing the Department of Agriculture, there to teach farming techniques and irrigation methods. Don and his team used this story everywhere they went. It was a good cover in case the authorities in the communities they were in questioned them. It was already getting late and night was falling. So, they grabbed dinner together in the hotel, making a point of not talking about the mission and just taking in the local flavor. There would be time for that tomorrow.

The next morning they met their contact, Raul, at the hotel restaurant. At first, he seemed nervous speaking to the three gringos. Don supposed in a place like this just talking to Americans might get Raul in trouble. But, a big breakfast helped him to calm down. He knew the gringos were paying the bill so he loaded up. Finally, they cut the small talk and began speaking quietly. Raul confirmed Gongo was the target.

"He is easy to get to since he fears nothing or no one in San Salvador," he said.

Out of nowhere another guy appeared in the restaurant, noticed Raul and quickly came over to sit down at the table. In a hushed tone he said,

"We've got two cars ready to go." Raul slid the keys casually across the table to Don.

"A white Honda and a gray Honda. They're right outside the door."

He continued, "The weapons, AK-47s, are sterilized and ready to go when you need them."

He handed them three cell phones. The phones were temporary phones purchased from street vendors in San Salvador. They were activated by purchasing minutes and were completely anonymous. These phones would be the only phones used during the operation and would be destroyed so they couldn't be traced once the mission was accomplished.

It was time to get the day started. Based on the information from Raul, they headed into the highlands and located

Gongo. They followed him for two days as he made his rounds in San Salvador. Don and Bob were one team and Manny and Raul switched off with them, using the other car when they got tired or felt Gongo saw them following him. This time was probably the most important of the whole mission. They needed to get to know Gongo's routines and the routes he took during his day trips. He drove a sleek black BMW, and to make sure they could tail him at night, Don used a trick he'd learned years ago doing night surveillance in the police department. When Gongo stopped at a restaurant one night, Don snuck up to his car, took out an ice pick and punctured a small hole in the red glass cover of the brake lights, without breaking it completely. Gongo would never notice the hole in the little plastic light cover, but to someone following him from behind it would appear as a stream of bright white light, allowing the team to keep their distance but remain aware of where his car was at all times.

The number one priority was the safety of the team before, during, and after the hit. The number two priority was to find a spot along the road for the hit that was sparsely populated, so bullets would not injure private citizens. The bad guys could care less who they shot—women, children, or old men—nothing mattered to them. But, the team wanted to know where all of their own bullets were going. They didn't want the deaths of innocents on their hands, and it helped them to justify the shootings in their own minds. Of course, priority three was the death of the intended target. The government determined this person had it coming to him, and the trio would follow those orders. After all, Don, Bob, and Manny all felt the same way; the only thing these bastards did was take up the air needed by other, good people.

The team found a secure location for Gongo to meet his demise. The plan was to strike him on the third day in San Salvador at approximately 10:30 a.m. when they knew he would be heading to one of his regular appointments. Sure enough, at that time Manny and Bob spotted Gongo's car leaving his house. Immediately the plan went into action, but after following him for a short distance the son of a bitch took another route and was lost in traffic.

They lost him until later that day. He was located again at 5:30 p.m., hanging out with some of his homeboys drinking it up at an outside bar near his house. They were harassing the women who walked by and laughing at their own jokes. There were too many people around and it didn't look like the situation would get any better. Rather than improvise with a crowd of drunken cartel thugs, it was best to stick to the plan already made and hope Gongo stuck to his routine tomorrow. Though disappointed, the team was more determined than ever to start again the next day.

On the fourth day, the team took up position down the street from his home at 7 a.m. They weren't going to miss another opportunity to get this son of a bitch. Don and Bob sat in the car for two hours under the scorching sun, beating off flies as big as cows, with sweat pouring off them.

Finally, Gongo came out of his driveway in the BMW. Don called Manny in the second car and told them to set up at the prearranged location. Both the cars had the AK-47s stashed in the back seats. Don and Bob followed two hundred feet behind Gongo's car, always letting the second car know their location.

Everything was going right. About a mile out of town, at the prearranged location, the second car had stopped at an intersection and opened the hood as if they were having engine trouble. Manny and Raul were out of the car staring at the engine compartment. They waved a hand at Gongo to get his attention. Gongo pulled up behind them and stopped. Manny started walking around the back of his car and towards Gongo, shouting in Spanish that they had overheated their car. Just as Gongo was about to go around them, Manny and Raul leapt into action and grabbed the loaded AK-47s from the back seat. They emptied all sixty rounds into Gongo's BMW. Don hit the gas.

There was no chance for Gongo. It was over in a few seconds. It had gone perfectly. There was no traffic on the road and there were no witnesses. Both cars sped away leaving the bullet riddled smoking heap of Gongo's car on the side of the road. About a mile from the Santa Rosa Hotel both of the cars stopped and the team put the AK-47s, the clips, the phones, and the gloves they had been wearing into one of the cars. The car sped away, driven by the nameless man from the café the day before, who had appeared from out of nowhere. No one ever knew this mysterious guy who had made it all happen and they never saw him again.

Raul drove Don, Bob, and Manny back to the Rosa Hotel. Raul was very thankful and shook everyone's hand. He quickly made himself scarce too. To Don it seemed like bad planning, and he didn't like it, but they couldn't leave San Salvador until the next morning. It was a long and very nervous night at the hotel. They knew the death of Gongo would be big news in the community, but they felt certain no one would think of them. No one had really noticed their presence anyway; they kept very low, speaking to very few people outside of the group. They were confident the hit made it look like a rival gang had killed Gongo. Besides, there were plenty of people who would be happy to see him dead. It was likely no one would care who had done it anyway.

It wasn't so bad flying back in to Phoenix with Bob and Manny. Of course, they didn't talk about the mission and it helped that they had their share of cocktails to pass the time. Bob and Manny left together and Don took a cab home to Mesa.

The mission was accomplished. It was time again for Don to process what had happened on his own. It was a fragile time for Don. Inevitably he would get to thinking and wondering whether what they had done was right. He always started questioning what he was doing when he was coming down from the high adrenaline rush of a mission.

Peter and the higher-ups in government had made the decision to eliminate Gongo. Don and his partners were simply soldiers carrying out orders. Just like in Vietnam. Just like on the police force. Don was following orders. But, these orders were different than the others. These orders required him to kill a man who was just going about his life. Sure, the man's life was worthless and did nothing but cause harm to good people, but Don would never take killing a human being in stride. He needed to feel it was the right thing to do and a last resort. When he first took on this type of work, he was told the reasons for such drastic actions. These guys were untouchable. He had to believe this was true.

He did trust his government and he did believe in his missions. But, he was human and doubts and second-guessing were part of the territory. He knew it would pass as things calmed down. He knew a few days of boring and a few nights with a bottle of wine would keep the demons at bay. He also knew it would be easier if he could talk about it with Diana, if he could be completely honest with her about where he had been and why. She was his best friend and she loved him. She would probably understand. He longed to open up about his double life with her or with his sons. But instead, for the next few weeks Don would be pretending like nothing ever happened and that was the real son of a bitch.

Chapter 7
COLUMBIA

SIX MONTHS HAD passed since Don's last trip out of the country. He thought maybe Peter and the others had forgotten about him until one afternoon, soon after arriving home from the golf course, the phone rang. Right away Don knew. It was Peter asking him to come to the Hilton Hotel the next day for some additional training. He gave Don the room number and the time to be there.

"Here we go," Don thought, not sure how he really felt about it.

When Don arrived he went straight to the room and knocked on the door. Manny Perez was already there and he was the one who answered. He greeted Don with a hearty handshake. Inside, Peter was sitting on a sofa with his laptop opened on the coffee table in front of him. Bob Kiser sat beside him and gave Don a nod. Peter got right to the point.

"Gentlemen, we need you to go to Colombia, South America. There's a person of interest there that needs dealing with immediately. His name is Manuel Vasquez Castillia. He is a captain in the El Norte Cartel. El Norte deals in large-scale exportation of cocaine to Europe and the United States. Castillia is a violent and very dangerous individual. He has been on the FBI's most wanted list for some time for the execution-style murders of two DEA agents in Miami. He's personally responsible for several kidnappings and extortion of foreigners visiting South America. He stays on the run most of the time, that's why we haven't been able to take care of him, but recently our informant there identified him and his place of residence in a poor section of Bogotá. He appears to be living alone and may even be hiding himself. We were waiting to see if he'd be taken out by another group, maybe someone he crossed, but time has run out. So gentlemen, we have to move fast and take this maniac off the streets before we lose track of him again. We don't have much else to go on and we need any ideas of how to eliminate him and make it look like an accident."

"Run him down with a car." Manny said.

"Won't work. Too risky. It sounds like he's in a populated area. There would be witnesses and it might be hard to get away. We'd probably be in a stolen car too. That could get messy for us if we get caught with a stolen car," Bob Kiser injected.

Don thought for a moment. He remembered a movie he recently saw.

"We could break in and make it appear to be an auto-erotic asphyxiation right in his own home. We could probably be in and out and there wouldn't be a sound. We wouldn't even need to shoot him. No blood. No mess."

Autoerotic asphyxiation was by all accounts a strange way to die. Often the victims don't intend to die, but it is a hazard of the act. It involves the restriction of oxygen to the brain during masturbation, which increases sexual arousal. The people who get involved in this kind of sex play say they get more of an intense orgasm just before they black out, from basically almost strangling themselves. Most of the time people induce autoerotic asphyxiation by bending their knees and hanging themselves from a doorframe with a belt or a tie. Then they masturbate until they orgasm. The idea is they can simply stand up after they climax and stop the suffocation. But often, they are so disoriented from a lack of oxygen that they can't stand up. If they go too far, even by accident, they black out and die. Thousands of people die each year from autoerotic asphyxiation. Don had read about it.

But, autoerotic asphyxiation wasn't too well known to anyone, even the police. And to the untrained eye of a police officer, it is often mistaken for suicide; nobody looks at this type of death as a homicide. It was the perfect way for this bastard to go. His family would be so ashamed at finding him with his pants down and porno magazines everywhere they wouldn't be telling too many people the truth of what happened, and they certain wouldn't be looking for anyone to have done it to him.

"That could work. Great idea, Don you make the plan," Peter said.

The meeting ended.

This one happened fast. The following Tuesday the three men left from Phoenix Sky Harbor airport to Mexico City where they would catch another flight to Colombia. Don had put the plan together in his mind, and before he left his house he stole a pair of his wife's panties, cut the label out of them so they wouldn't be traceable and threw it away. When they arrived in Mexico City, Don bought two Mexican porn magazines with graphic pictures at the airport. They went on to Colombia that night, grabbed a taxi and a bite to eat at the hotel, and waited out the night in their separate hotel rooms.

As usual, they were met the next day by their contact, who set them up with a car and weapons. Don didn't anticipate needing the weapons on this trip, but they were good to have just the same. They had an address given to them by Peter and a vehicle description. It took a while to get their bearings on the chaotic streets of Bogotá, but they located Castillia's apartment building and found his car in the parking lot.

They spent some time casing the place to figure out his patterns. Every place, everyone has a pattern. This was part of the work. You had to have the patience to sit, watch, and wait before you got down to business. If you didn't have this patience you could make mistakes and easily end up dead yourself. Don used the time to go over the plan with Manny and Bob and to review how it was going to go down. They were all anxious to get this one over with since it would involve actually entering the guy's house. Usually they did the hit out in the open when the guy was heading out or heading home. The last thing they wanted was to feel like trapped rats in Bogotá, Columbia. They decided they would strike early in the morning. It looked like Castillia lived alone and after following him home that night they were sure he was the only one there.

About 5:30 a.m., just before sunrise, Don and Bob hid, and Manny knocked on Castillia's apartment door. Castillia opened the door to see who was out there so early in the morning. He wasn't even cautious, which Don would later remember. This guy wasn't afraid of anyone. He thought he was safe. Don and Bob rushed in with Manny right behind them and they threw Castillia on the floor, knocking over a chair and end table. They stuck a rag in his mouth Don had grabbed from the back of the taxi.

"Don't move or we'll kill you," Don said as he shoved his knee harder into Castillia's chest.

They worked quickly. Manny went into the bedroom, found a silk tie in the closet, and returned. While Don and Bob held him down, Manny wrapped the tie around Castillia's neck and strangled him right then and there. They took his body into the bedroom, being careful not to harm it any way that would cause suspicion. The tie was still around his neck as they lifted the body up, securing the tie on a closet rail. Castillia was hanging with his knees approximately five to six inches off the ground. His shins and his feet were bent back on the floor. He looked like a man who had just hung himself.

They immediately took off his pajama pants and his underwear and threw the clothes on the bed. Don pulled his wife's stolen panties on Castillia's legs up to his knees. He then took the two porno books, opened them up, and laid them on the floor beneath him. They left the closet doors open so the hanging body was easily visible. The three straightened up the front room so there was no sign of struggle. They locked all the windows and locked the front door from the inside so there would be no suspicion that someone had broken in and killed Castillia. They left as quietly as they had come. No one saw them. No one heard them.

Anyone investigating this death would have to rule it either a suicide or an autoerotic asphyxiation. A novice investigator would rule it a suicide. Very few, especially down here, would know about autoerotic asphyxiation and determine that is what happened. Regardless of which way they ruled the death, they'd be too busy to even consider it a homicide. There simply wasn't enough evidence left behind by Don and the guys. This was exactly how they wanted it to appear.

Relatively speaking, Don thought this had been a pretty easy and stress free mission. If they were all like this, maybe he would keep doing it.

They dropped the car with the weapons in the trunk at the designated spot and were driven back to wait out the rest of the day and night at the hotel. This was the hard part. Don would have liked nothing more than to get the hell out of the country as fast as possible. He didn't like hanging around and waiting for flights.

Don met up with Bob at the hotel bar at dinnertime. A couple of beers and a good steak dinner would help to pass the time.

"Where's Manny?" Don asked.

Bob paused then let out a sarcasm-laden chuckle.

"Oh, he's out having some fun."

Don instantly became uneasy.

"What do you mean? Out where? In town?"

"Not really in town."

Bob's answer was cryptic and Don felt the agitation rising. He was the de facto head of this mission and the fact that Manny's whereabouts were unknown, at least by Don himself, was pissing him off. They were a team, and the team needed to know everything about each other. The team needed to have each other's backs, and they couldn't do that if one of them disappeared without telling the others.

"Bob, where the hell is Manny?" Don did not hide his agitation.

"Look Don. It's a long story. Manny didn't think you'd notice if he was gone for the night. I don't really care, but I'm not gonna lie for him."

"So ... "

"He's with a woman."

"What woman? A prostitute?"

"No. At least I don't think so. Who knows. It's a woman he met on another trip. He's been down here a few times. He thinks he's in love or some shit like that."

Don nearly knocked his beer over as he turned to face Bob full on.

"Are you telling me Manny is having an affair with a woman down here? Are you really telling me that?"

"That's what I'm telling you." Bob resigned himself to being the bearer of the bad news.

"Jesus Christ! This is just great. We could be fucked already and not even know it. What the hell is he thinking? He's out there, in country, fucking around on his wife and putting his name and face all over the place. Who the hell is she? Who does she know? Ah Jesus, this is bad."

"I know. I know. It could be bad. I didn't know about it until tonight and there was no talking him out of going over to her house. He's thinking of leaving Maria for her. He's not thinking straight and I told him so."

Don did not enjoy his dinner. The beers did nothing to calm his nerves or make the night go any faster. He wanted to get the hell out of here as fast as possible, especially now, but there was no way to speed up time. There was no way of finding Manny, and there was no way of making this OK. He'd have to deal with Manny in the morning and get through the night the best he could.

Don and Bob had a long history and they also shared a certain sense of right and wrong, especially when it came to these missions. Manny had let them down and Don wasn't sure what to think about it. He couldn't think about the big picture right now anyway. All he could do was make sure that they all, or at least he and Bob, got out of Colombia safely, with no hassles.

In the morning, they met in the lobby for the shuttle van to the airport. Don was silent and Manny must have guessed Don knew. But Don didn't want to make a scene in the hotel. He'd wait until they were in private and then try to set Manny straight.

The van ride was the perfect opportunity.

"Hey Manny, why don't you sit in the back with me and Bob can ride shotgun," Don said as the van pulled up under the portico.

Bob took signals well and knew his job was to distract the driver so Don could have a little chat with Manny.

When they were well under way, the noisy van, as well as Bob's chattering, shielded Don's voice from the driver. He spoke in a low tone, not yelling, not angry, but in a way that Manny would have no misunderstanding about Don's true feelings.

"If you ever do that again, you're out. In fact, you may be out anyway. I haven't decided yet. Your actions last night put all of us in danger. Serious danger. You compromised the mission. You compromised my life and you compromised Bob's life. I have a wife. I have kids. I have grandkids. And I will not work with someone who has such poor judgment. Have an affair if you want to, but don't do it when I'm around."

"Don, I'm sorry." Manny started to explain himself. "It's not what you think. She's not just anyone. I know her. She knows she cannot tell anyone about me. No one saw me. No one knows. Except for you and Bob now."

"I don't care Manny. No one is safe outside of us three. No one. No exceptions. Ever. That's how it has to be and if you don't like it, you're done."

"OK. OK. I'm sorry. I get it. I let my emotions get the better of me. I just wanted to see her. "

"Well, that's a whole different topic and one I don't think you want my opinion on."

"I know. I know. I'm in a mess."

"No. You're not in a mess. You're being stupid. You have a great wife. You have great kids. A home. A great life. Why are you putting it all at risk? What for? If you're just bored with the sex, go get a prostitute. This is ridiculous, not to mention potentially deadly."

"I know. I'm sorry. I have to figure this out."

"Damn right you do. What we do is hard and dangerous enough. I don't need someone around who makes bad decisions based on their emotions. And, I don't need some Colombian thug coming after me because of you. Think about it. Think about someone other than yourself."

"OK Don. I'm really sorry. I'll get this figured out and you will never hear about it again. It will never come into play again."

"Good."

That was Don's final word. He'd let it go for now. There was no sense in belaboring the point today, but his trust and faith in Manny were now destroyed. Don wasn't sure he'd be able to do another mission with him. If he did another mission that was.

They arrived at the airport, went through the slipshod security screening, and boarded a plane back to the United States. When the plane lifted off, Don finally relaxed, at least a little bit. All three were sitting on the plane. Nobody was saying a word, so to break the tension Manny said,

"Hey Don, I knew you would kill anyone that got into your wife's panties."

It worked. Don didn't hold grudges. He had said his piece to Manny and now they would move on. They all had a good laugh and the crude comments went around. The wine helped of course.

They parted ways in Miami and Don went back to Phoenix. Though this mission had been a little easier than the others, with the exception of the problems with Manny, Don still felt the same let down. Back at home, things were normal. The days were ticking by the way they always did and Don felt the frustration of not being able to just blurt out where he had been. When Diana started asking questions he answered with the usual bullshit about transporting illegals back to their own country instead of saying, "I just flew to Bogotá for a few days, killed some asshole drug lord and then set up a fake autoerotic asphyxiation to make it look like he killed himself."

Jesus! They'd put him in the psych ward if he said that. So once again, Don went through a period of feeling bad about not being able to discuss his double life with anyone. He felt the anxiety again of waiting for someone to come knocking on his door. It was tough for him not knowing who knew what he had done, not knowing if some government guy would come and arrest him or some terrorist would somehow track him down. There was no debriefing, no thank you. No one ever contacted him after his missions. He was alone.

Chapter 8
NO TIME FOR DOUBTS

A QUIET COUPLE of months passed after the Columbia mission. Don and Diana were going about their days, Don enjoying his so-called retirement. They socialized with friends every weekend and cookouts were always part of the plan. It was April and Easter was late this year, but just around the corner. This was the time of year when Arizona began to empty out. Easter was the dividing line between those who were in the desert for the long haul of summer and those who were living the snowbird lifestyle. Don didn't mind the heat. In fact, he kind of liked it once he figured out it was just a matter of changing your lifestyle. When it started to get over one hundred degrees, it was time to shut things down in the afternoons, have a siesta, just like they did in Mexico. They knew what they were doing down there, south of the border. Anyone who went to Safeway, or out to run any errands, during the brutal mid-afternoon sun of summer was crazy. From lunchtime to five o'clock was the time for catching up on paperwork and laying low until the sun started its descent for the day. Dinner was later in the summer. Bedtime was later in the summer, but in this way, the heat was tolerable. Don even enjoyed the shift in lifestyle. After all, summer nights in the desert were spectacular: warm, dry and no bugs.

Don and Diana were going to attend Easter sunrise services with visiting friends from Chicago. His old partner on the Chicago police force was arriving in two weeks. Don was looking forward to seeing him. The only glitch in the excitement was the guy's wife was a holy roller. Don would have to be careful and watch his mouth and not drink too much around her. Hopefully she would go to bed early and leave the guys to their reminiscing.

On Saturday night the home telephone rang and Diana answered it.

"It's for you honey, they didn't say who it was."

Don immediately felt the rush go through him. No one ever called him on the landline phone anymore; it seemed only telemarketers ever called this number now. He had thought about getting rid of it altogether, but there was still one important person who contacted Don this way. So, the sudden rush was understandable.

Diana handed him the phone.

"Don, how are you?"

"Hey buddy. I'm okay, how about you?" Don started small talk while he slipped out to the patio and out of Diana's earshot.

"Meet me tomorrow in Veteran's Park by the fountain at two o'clock. The team will be there," was all Peter said.

"OK, I'll be there," Don stammered before he could even think twice. It was like he was hardwired to spit out an automatic yes to these requests. Despite the previous month's second thoughts and doubts about whether he wanted to do this anymore, here he was again, going to be briefed on a mission. He cursed himself for jumping so quickly. He already knew whatever Peter wanted would be dangerous and would require his full attention for at least a couple of weeks to come. His mind started racing, and as the adrenaline rush kicked in, he headed back into the house for a glass of wine.

At the designated date and time Don headed to Veteran's Park. He spotted Bob Kiser sitting at a picnic table. The two buddies greeted each other with a hardy handshake. Despite Don's misgivings, it was always nice to see Bob.

"So where's the mystery man?"

As usual, Don tried to lighten his own mood with a little humor.

"Ah, he'll be here. You know how prompt he always is. He has a few minutes. "

Then, as expected Peter arrived with briefcase in hand and sat down on the other side of the picnic table. As usual, he wasted no time on pleasantries and got right to the point of the meeting.

"Gentlemen. As you know, Puerto Rico is a U.S territory and will likely someday become a state. For those reasons, what goes on there concerns us. One of our informants has given us information about a drug ring operating there that is shipping thousands of kilos of cocaine out to Europe. Mostly to Spain and Italy."

Don cut in, "It doesn't sound like our problem since it goes overseas."

"That may be so, but it is in our best interest to show

our authority in Puerto Rico. In addition, both Spain and Italy have asked for our assistance in stopping the flow. The territory today has its share of the usual gangs dealing in drugs, prostitution, and black market products. But, there is one corporation in particular, North Star Shipping, which we know has a hand in the biggest of the drug shipments. We've had them under surveillance for the past ten months, so we're pretty confident at this point."

Bob broke in, "So, why not let DEA go in and bust them then? Why us?"

"Not an option. They're smart and savvy, and the owners hide behind a well-constructed wall of paperwork and law-yers. Everything is legit—on the surface."

"So how does this North Star Shipping operate? How do they do it?"

Peter, as always, was well equipped with answers.

"It's a father and son operation. Carlos and Fernando or 'Nano' Ortiz run the show. Carlos is 60 and Nano is only 24, but you won't find their names on anything concerning North Star. Both are connected to a Colombian cartel that supplies the drugs."

Peter reached across the picnic table and handed them recent photos of the two men in question.

"Nano, the son, runs their operation in Puerto Rico. On paper, they're supposed to be importers and exporters. They run a couple of warehouses on the island. That's the front. The behind-the-scenes business is booming and they have the capability to ship worldwide. Nano is just a piece of shit punk. At 19 he was convicted of selling cocaine in New York and spent three years in prison at Attica where he was nothing but a troublemaker. Most of his teen years were spent in juvenile detention centers for assault, attempted murder, possession, and auto theft. He was raised in the Bronx and was in a gang of course, so God knows what else he's done. Those are just the things he got caught for. Now he lives, in Puerto Rico full-time. He hasn't changed much. Down there he travels with a bunch of thugs, his posse. The drug business has made him rich, but he continues to pretty much terrorize those around him. His ego is huge and that means he'll stop at nothing to preserve his lifestyle. I'm telling you all of this so you know the complete situation down there, but Nano is not your primary concern."

Don and Bob shot each other a sideways glance. How much worse could the father be?

Peter continued, "Now, the father, Carlos Ortiz is another story. Carlos runs the operation from the Dominican Republic. I'll be blunt. He is one dangerous motherfucker. He takes no bullshit from anyone. Our sources have seen him have guys killed for making a smart remark at the wrong time. His time in the U.S. ended when he was deported several years back for second-degree murder, several assault charges, and a long list of assorted other felonies. He ended up in the DR and now runs North Star from a small port on the southeast side of the island, near Punta Cana. He's considered a businessman down there and he has a horse ranch in the highlands. He entertains his clients and puts on his show as a perfect gentleman on the outside, but make no mistake, he's a real son of a bitch on the inside. One thing that might be helpful is that he's a member of the Bayside Country Club where he entertains and plays golf."

There are many reasons why Ortiz chose the Dominican Republic to run his drug pipeline overseas. Of course, money talks in the DR and there's multiple layers of corruption in law enforcement, the government, lawyers and even judges. Just about everyone down there is on the take if the right amount is offered. So, of course it's very easy for him to get customs agents to look the other way when North Star ships pass through the port, despite our presence. The U.S. has an FBI office, a DEA office, an ambassador with staff and other agencies operating there, but still the web of corruption is wide and deep and North Star has penetrated it well at all levels. My advice to you is to trust no one there. Even our own."

That was the background. Don and Bob took a minute to absorb all Peter had just dumped on them. Don had the fleeting observation that because he was so absorbed listening to Peter and in analyzing the situation—how it worked, who the players were, how a plan could be made—that he hadn't entertained any of the doubts he had been carrying around for months. For good or bad, this stuff made him tick.

Well, he was in it now.

"So, explain how the shipments work." Don dove in.

"Okay. So, when North Star has a ship that will be going to Spain or Italy it leaves out of Puerto Rico with a partial load of sugar or rice, and other products. Once they reach international waters they meet up with drug runners from various places in South America, mostly Colombia, and take on the drugs from that boat. They store them as cargo in the exact bags as the sugar or rice, not a new trick really. But, then they head to the DR, and they may take on more drugs at Ortiz's port there. Because of the payoffs, customs looks the other way and off they go to Europe. Spain and Italy are the destinations because of their own notoriously lax cargo inspections."

"Makes sense," Don said. "Now what do you want us to do?"

"Well, it's tricky. Carlos and Nano are the lynchpins so we want the father and the son taken out at the same time on the same day. Nice and quiet. No opportunities for warnings or for hiding. And we definitely don't want an international incident."

Don was silent for a moment. This was a new twist, and a pretty crazy one he thought. Simultaneous hits in different countries. Finally, it came out.

"How in the hell can we do that, one in Puerto Rico and the other in DR, and why for God's sake?"

"Like I said. We can't have one alert the other when we take care of the first one. Otherwise, it's all for nothing. If one hears about the other's death, he'll run to South America, hide out till it's safe and then just set up shop again. They know how to do it. They have the money to restart and the guys they pay off to make it happen will be waiting with open arms to get their kickbacks again. We might stop it for a month or two if we take out one, but what we're going for here is a complete end to the pipeline. Their deaths will do that. They're tight and don't have lieutenants to step up and take over if something happens to them."

"Well, this is going to take some serious planning and coordination." Don was already stressing, as he knew the major planning would fall on his shoulders.

"I'm thinking you can make it look like a rival gang or even that the Colombians did it. A deal gone bad, you know. I want you and Bob to go to the DR and take out Carlos. I've got Manny and another guy briefed for the trip to Puerto Rico to take care of little Nano. Communications between the countries are pretty good. It will take some doing to figure out how to coordinate their comings and goings, but once the date and time are set the two teams should be able to communicate by cell phone and in code to know when the job is done."

Don was shaking his head, "I don't see how it can be the exact minute, things don't work that way."

Peter smiled, "OK, let's say a thirty minute window. The point is that we can't have a call going out to either one, from anyone, saying the other is dead."

"OK, let me get started on the research and see what I can come up with." Don paused.

"Geez. These things just keep getting crazier and crazier. So, what's the time line? When do we fly out? I need a few days to pull it together."

"No problem. You and Bob will fly commercial to the DR and land in Punta Cana this Tuesday. You're gonna be there for five days to play golf and relax so dress the part. The cover is a little different on this one so take golf clubs with you and of course you'll have a car. Local contacts will get it set up with weapons, likely they'll be in the trunk under the spare tire. The rest is per usual. After the hit return the car with weapons inside to the designated spot and they'll be destroyed. I've arranged for two knives, an Uzi, and a P13 with silencer. You'll each have a throw away cell phone. Anything else you need?"

Don smirked. Peter knew his stuff. "No boss, that'll get the job done."

He handed Don a file folder as he stood up to leave.

"You've got all the information in there on both Carlos and Nano. Once you're there, we'll get you hooked up with Manny's cell for coordination. Be sure to destroy that file once you've read it. Good luck men. And speedy return."

If we return that is, Don thought.

Chapter 9
DOMINICAN REPUBLIC

DRESSED IN TROPICAL attire, Don and Bob arrived at the Punta Cana International Airport along with two dozen raucous golfers. It was still cold enough in the U.S. that the tropics were the place to be. Warm breezes, short-sleeved shirts and a day on the links next to the sea was just what the tourists were looking for. Punta Cana is known for at least a dozen first class golf courses and Don and Bob had no problem fitting right into the crowd. When they exited the terminal a local approached them and handed them a set of keys. Slightly surprised, but knowing this was likely the drop off, Don didn't ask any questions. He just took the keys and said thanks as the man pointed to a white Lexus SUV parked along the curb. Don and Bob put their luggage in the back, but not before first lifting the spare tire to make sure everything was going according to the plan. The package was there. They'd look at it closer later. They headed to the Bavaro Palace Resort in Punta Cana. This was one of those high-end, luxury, no-kids-allowed resorts. Don had to admit he felt a little too much like he was on vacation and not here to do a job. Maybe this was the government's way of keeping him on the payroll. If so, it was working. After checking in to their rooms they headed to the bar to discuss the mission.

"This sure is a fancy place for the likes of you and me," Bob said looking at the pristine white beach lined with palm trees. "Don't get any romantic ideas."

Don just chuckled. "Yup, Uncle Sam isn't gonna like the tab we run up here," he said as he ordered two top-shelf margaritas from the young, and of course, gorgeous girl behind the bar.

"So, have you thought about how we're gonna get on this asshole?" Bob asked, after a toast with his margarita.

"Well, we know where to find him so a couple of days of surveillance should give us a good idea of his routines. We know where he lives and the port office is only a few miles away so we'll start there to see if he goes to the office every day. I'm sure he has security at both places, so we'll have to find their holes. If we have to, we can shoot the fucker at a distance, but it would be cleaner to just slit his throat in close quarters and walk away quietly. That's the way I always prefer it at least." Don sounded like the old pro that he was.

"That will give a little more time for the guys in Puerto Rico, in case the timing's off. We're booked here for five days so we have plenty of time to get to know the situation. We can't do it too early because we have to ride it out after the hit until our flight leaves. We can't make any waves by trying to leave early. I don't want to try to hide out here either and I definitely don't want to be sitting around waiting for a knock at the door. I'd say the day before we leave which is Saturday would be a good day to send this bastard to hell."

"So, we'll watch and wait. Not a bad plan to pass the time," Bob said checking out the ass on a tight little young blonde walking by, wearing nothing but a bikini.

"We have to play some golf, you up for that?" Don grabbed Bob's attention back.

"I'm not a great golfer. I'll shoot in the hundreds if I'm lucky."

"OK, I need to find out where this Carlos Ortiz plays golf. Peter said he's a member of one of the high-end clubs here and plays every week with his big shot buddies. I'm sure people will know him. We might even be able to isolate him on the course."

Don was thinking the golf course would be an option for taking him out.

They ordered another round of margaritas. One thing was sure, staying in Punta Cana with all of its fabulous resorts, spas, beaches, casinos, booze, and women meant Don was going to have a hard time staying focused.

"Let's leave the weapons where they are for now, but get the cell phones in case Manny has problems. I don't know about this timing issue. All we can do is our best."

Despite having one too many margaritas, they got up early and found Ortiz's house. It was in a quiet neighborhood of homes surrounded by eight-foot walls. The Ortiz hacienda had barbed wire running along the top. Typical. Don was pretty sure it wasn't going to happen here anyway.

At eight Ortiz left in a Mercedes SUV. They followed him down the coast highway towards the port. He pulled into a gated and fenced area and they watched as he went into a warehouse. The port area in Punta Cana was small but could easily accommodate two ships. This is where North Star's ships docked. Don and Bob scoped out the neighborhood and stayed close by until eleven, when Ortiz returned home.

They'd see if that was his daily routine tomorrow. In the afternoon, Don decided to check out the golf club Ortiz belonged to. They paid their non-member fees, plus a little extra, anything could be bought here, and got a late-afternoon tee time despite the crowds. In the clubhouse Bob was browsing through a brochure rack and spotted something interesting.

"Hey Don, check this out," he handed Don the brochure.

"Yeah, a pro-am golf tournament at the Teeth of the Dog course this weekend. Crazy name, but what about it?"

"Turn it over. Check out the sponsors listed on the back."

Don flipped to the back, not so thrilled with the search and find game. He read down the list, Presidente, Brugal, Hershey, Carnival, US Airways, North Star Shipping.

"Whoa! Holy shit," Don almost yelled. "These drug dealing cocksuckers are sponsoring this event?"

"It sure looks that way. Odds are our guy will be at that tournament. This just might be the place to do our job."

"Yeah, but with a few thousand spectators hanging around," Don sneered.

Bob pushed on, "But, the tournament is Friday, Saturday, and Sunday. Saturday is our deadline to get it done. We fly back early Sunday morning. It could work."

Don wasn't sure yet. "Alright. If we don't find another opportunity in the next two days this might be the only solution we have left. Good find."

"It might be hard to get tickets this late. We'll have to pull some strings. Maybe you'll have to use your golf course employee experience to snag us an insider's deal. Or just use your charming personality." Bob new this would get a rise out of Don.

Don smiled, "Okay, okay. But I really think this has to be our plan B, or even C. I'd rather not do this with so many witnesses around. By the way, even here, there's bound to be a lot of security at this kind of event with these kinds of big corporate sponsors."

"I get it. I think it's just worth looking into."

"Alright, now let's put on our party hats and play the part of tourist. It's time to do our duty and hit the beach and the bar. After all, we don't want to appear suspicious."

With that, they went about the hard work of blending in as tourists.

———————

Up early again the next day, they drove to the residential neighborhood where Ortiz had his mini-castle. The good news was he had the same routine. The bad news was he had security guards, both at his house and at the warehouse. Don entertained the idea of hitting him on the coastal highway as he was driving to the port, but there was usually quite a bit of traffic, which meant too many potential witnesses. Besides, the highway ran east and west, and not knowing the area, it would be hard to pick a suitable escape route in case they were seen. Don wasn't comfortable trying to outrun anyone in this place, being an island and all. Bob's idea of the golf tournament was beginning to look better and better. Who knows what Ortiz did in that office all day long, probably sat there counting his dirty money, but he sure didn't do much else. Assuming he was going to the tournament, it looked like that would have to be the plan. The hard part was coordinating it with the guys in Puerto Rico.

They went back to the resort and Don called Manny to see what things looked like on their end.

"We're shooting for Saturday early evening. How does that look for your guy?" Don asked Manny.

"Perfect. It turns out Nano is throwing a party Saturday night so we'll know exactly where he'll be. My partner is already in with a couple of his buddies, so we'll be there and I have no doubt I can make it happen on your word. "

Don finally admitted their only real play was to take Ortiz out at the tournament. The only obstacle now was the tickets. But, that was nothing that a few American dollars couldn't fix. With a little contribution to the cash economy of the island, through the hotel concierge, Don and Bob magically had last minute VIP tickets to the biggest event on the island that weekend.

With the plan now loosely in place Don and Bob took advantage of another night in paradise. Dinner by the sea and a few drinks at the bar put them both in a relaxed mood, even considering the circumstances. They weren't supposed to socialize too much on these trips. The less people they came into contact with, the better. It was a good thing they liked each other's company.

On Friday morning, they scoped out Carlos' house again, hoping for a break in the port office routine. They breathed a sigh of relief when he headed instead towards La Romana for the tournament. The game was on.

The tournament wasn't as crowded as Don had feared. This was the first day though. Surely the weekend would be busier. This was a good day to get the lay of the club and for Don to make the final plan. Today was all about information gathering. Don also got his first good long look at Carlos Ortiz. He was a greasy sort, a spare tire around the middle, slicked back jet-black hair and clothes that gave away his age. But what did he care? He had enough money and enough power in his own little world that he could be whoever he wanted to be. He didn't need to impress anyone. Everyone else was working at impressing him. Oddly enough, given his occupation, he was not surrounded by heavy security. There was one guy who hovered in the area, but he was a cinch to spot and could easily be taken care of. Don supposed Ortiz felt pretty safe in his island home, knowing the authorities, both Dominican and American were sufficiently paid off to leave him alone. Don had to chuckle at the innocence of such an otherwise savvy man.

They checked out the leader board. Carlos Ortiz was playing with a pro out of South Africa. They'd be teamed up together for the whole three days. Thankfully, Don's work at the Mesa golf course came in handy. He knew how long it would take to play the nine or eighteen holes and he could talk the talk to the staff around the course. Don got a look at the schedule when he was hanging around with the caddies. Carlos' tee time for Saturday was at three o'clock. That meant his foursome would arrive back at the clubhouse after the first nine at about five o'clock. They'd probably take a short break and then start the back nine holes. They'd finish up about seven o'clock since this was not real serious play. The timing was perfect. Don's plan was to make his move at the clubhouse. Surely there would be a time when Ortiz was alone, maybe in the bathroom. If not, he'd have him paged or called to the phone.

Don and Bob hung around for a while and watched a few rounds. Pro-am tournaments were pretty entertaining, depending on who was there of course. There weren't any real big names here, mostly lower-level players looking to spend the week around Easter on a warm and sunny island. After a few rounds of golf and beers they returned to Punta Cana and the resort. Sleep didn't come easy for Don that night. He really wasn't confident they could pull off this hit simultaneously with the team in Puerto Rico. Though he would strive to make the mission go as planned, he was more concerned with taking out his man than with the timing. If the timing didn't work, the government would have to deal with those consequences. But, if he botched up his end of the work because he was concerned with their timing issue, he would have to deal with the consequences, and those would likely be deadly. Fuck the timing he thought. If it works it works, if it doesn't, it doesn't. It was too much to ask anyway.

The real reason sleep wouldn't come was because of the anticipation of the actual act of taking a life. This is what weighed heavily on his mind. Sure, he had done it many times before, in Vietnam, and on other missions like this, but it never got easier. Even when he knew for himself that what he was doing was right, it still didn't make it easy.

Finally, around midnight he gave up on the tossing and turning and went to the bar. He ordered a double scotch and water to try and get relaxation straight to the source. It helped him calm down, so he ordered another. There were a few vacationers in the bar, who by this time were looking pretty happy. They didn't notice him. He was like a fly on the wall. His thoughts roamed to the next day and what he would have to do. It seems he always spent this time before a hit wrestling with his choices and coming to terms with them in his mind. He had taken the job voluntarily because this guy Ortiz was on his country's most-wanted list and they had no other way of stopping him. Both the father and the son had it coming to them, he reasoned. They had ruined enough lives and they had no good reason to stop dealing and masterminding one criminal scheme after the other in order to make themselves richer. Don was sure they never sat quietly at a bar far from home and thought about what they were doing, about the lives they were affecting, about the millions of people and families who were ruined because of the drugs they put on the streets. Don reasoned killing Ortiz was for the good of God and Country and that was good enough for him.

<hr/>

Showing his business card, Don managed to get into the clubhouse that afternoon as a guest. Bob was out on the course in the gallery watching Ortiz's foursome. Bob phoned Don on their progress.

By the time they got to the eighteenth hole, it was nearing seven o'clock. Timing was of the essence at this point. Bob reported Ortiz had parred the last hole. Well, Don thought, good for him. At least he ended on a high note and wasn't going to go meet his maker having to explain a bogie too.

Don caught sight of them as they came up the cartway in front of the clubhouse. They were all lighthearted, cracking jokes and laughing as they made their way into the restaurant for a celebratory dinner. The restaurant was busy with the tournament and Don was standing near the bar just waiting and watching. There were others waiting for the attention of the bartender too and he had no problem blending in. He had his knife and gun tucked away under his tropical tourist shirt. This was it. It was go time. Pretending to look at a menu, Don's senses were firing on all cylinders as he practically willed Ortiz to separate from the group. Before he knew it, it happened. Ortiz headed for the bathroom down a long corridor, while the others were looking at the leader board facing the lobby.

Don snapped into high gear. When Ortiz disappeared down the hall, Don quickly followed. As he entered, two other guys came out. They were in a heated discussion and barely noticed Don. He put his head down anyway and moved quickly so they wouldn't have a good look at him. When he pushed through the door, Ortiz was at the urinal. He didn't seem to notice or care and was just staring at the wall in front of him. Quickly, Don swept the room. No one was in the stalls so he didn't hesitate. Silently, smooth and swift as a panther, he slid the long knife out of his waistband, stepped behind Ortiz and plunged it into the scumbag's neck with a downward power stroke, just like he had learned in Vietnam. It never failed him. The knife sunk deep down through Ortiz's throat and into his lungs. He was immobilized, and on his way out fast. Don grabbed the body before it hit the floor and maneuvered it into a toilet stall. Moving quickly, but accurately, he put Ortiz's head into the commode and pulled his knife out. Instantly, blood filled the commode. Carlos bled out quickly. Don managed to remain spotless.

He exited the bathroom. Thankfully, no one was coming down the hall. He passed the rest of Ortiz's foursome at the entrance to the restaurant, still eyeing the leaderboard. Sorry to ruin your game fellas, he thought, but it will sure be one to remember. He strolled calmly outside into another beautiful evening in paradise. He was sure no one had noticed him, although there were a hundred people in the clubhouse. The whole thing had taken less than three minutes.

Don called Bob who was parked nearby with the SUV already running. He hopped in the passenger's seat, letting Bob drive this leg.

"Let's get the hell out of here slowly. It's over. It went like clockwork."

"Where is he now?" Bob asked.

"Let's just say he's eating shit right now."

That was it. They phoned the other team in Puerto Rico and informed them of the demise of Ortiz the elder. It turned out Manny had just finished up too. But, now wasn't the time to compare notes. In fact, they would probably never compare notes. It was enough for Don to know they had actually pulled off a near simultaneous hit in two different countries. Despite the messiness of this business and all the bad feelings that came along with it, he loved the thrill of it and now this added bonus of precision timing.

They headed back to the resort and took a swim. The bar was their friend and they did the usual thing of not talking about the events of the afternoon. That was fine with Don. He knew he'd have a whole lot of time later to go over it again and again. He was fine with just enjoying his margaritas and heading into oblivion. The nightly news came on the television at the bar. There was coverage of the tournament and Don and Bob watched intently, but there was nothing about what had happened. It must have been too late to get the story in. By the time it hit the news, they'd be long gone. Thankfully, they had a 6 a.m. flight to catch and they'd be on their way to Miami in a few short hours. Don would be home for Easter after all.

Chapter 10

THE MOTHER OF ALL MISSIONS

IT WAS MID-NOVEMBER before Don got another phone call from Peter. He was asked to join the team for a training session the next day, this time back at the Hilton Hotel. Don agreed and it was easy to slip out to the Hilton while Diana was at work. He went to the room number Peter had given him. When he entered, he immediately saw this gathering was different from the previous sessions. Manny and Bob were seated on the sofa near the window. Peter was seated in the upholstered chair with his laptop on the coffee table, as usual. But, behind Peter stood two suits Don didn't recognize. They were the silent and stoic types, with hard-set jaws and Ray Bans tucked into their collars. They stood at ease, but looked ready for anything. Don suspected they were Secret Service or CIA. After the initial greetings, Peter began his usual instructions to the three.

He began, "OK. First thing. I want each of you to know this mission is very different from the others you've been on so far. It is going to involve a lot more upfront planning and will take you out of the country for several weeks. This is a dangerous, but extremely important mission, and if any one of you feels like you are not up to it, let me know anytime during this meeting. There will be no hard feelings if you decide to step out."

Don froze up a little. He had gotten used to the almost routine nature of the previous missions. In and out. Fast and furious. Even the mission down in the Dominican Republic, though more complicated than the others, was over pretty fast. Well, he knew he wouldn't back out, but he was a little unnerved that he seemed to be getting in deeper than he already was with his new line of work.

The suits had come with Peter moved out of their statue-like positions and handed each man a folder containing photos, maps, and other data. Don flipped through his. A map of Venezuela, a picture of a priest, satellite images of a compound in the mountains and pages and pages of detailed information; what the heck were they getting into he wondered.

"Here's the situation." Peter began.

"We want you to go to Caracas, Venezuela in two weeks. Don, you will be traveling undercover as a priest and you will head the operation. Manny and Bob will back you up in any way necessary to get the job done. Your mission is to destroy a complex run by a notorious international criminal named Bernard Kroslak, and to eliminate him too."

Don, Manny, and Bob studied the paperwork in the folders. Don could feel the tension in the room. It was different than before. There was no joking around this time.

Peter continued, "Kroslak is a flamboyant, well-mannered,

educated, and shrewd businessman. He is also a cold-blood-ed killer. Many of the Mexican and South American cartels funnel their money through the operations he's built up all over the globe. He mainly deals in the sale of illegal weapons around the world. In the eighties, he got into the cocaine business and he made billions. Now, he has a lot of influ-ence. At heart, he's a businessman. He even convinced many of his cartel friends to go legitimate with the billions they had accumulated, though he's never taken the advice himself. The operation is very high-tech and sophisticated. Kroslak's operation can deliver everything from tanks to missiles, ar-tillery, small arms, and helicopters. Wherever the client is, whatever the client wants, he can deliver. He doesn't dis-criminate in his clients either. If they have the money, he'll deliver the goods. He caters to the worst of humanity: dicta-tors, the cartels, fanatical groups in the Middle East like the Taliban, and African warlords.

Just to give you an idea of how this guy operates, he re-cently sent caches of small arms to a maniac warlord in Nigeria who proceeded to murder hundreds of people, in one day, in his own province. Kroslak knew who the guy was and his likely intentions with the weapons, but the money was too good to pass up. His armaments are manufactured by connec-tions all over the world, in China, Russia, Pakistan, Bulgaria, and Poland. But, the one group he avoids dealing with is the United States, and he has a general hatred for the American way of life. This makes Venezuela, which already has it out for the U.S., the perfect place from which to base his whole operation. In fact, he's likely in with the Venezuelan govern-ment, arming them with whatever they need.

Kroslak even has access to missile launchers that could be a real threat to the United States if they get into the wrong hands. He's still just a thug though and under his orders, his security team has killed hundreds of people who have gotten in his way: police, politicians, sometimes friends. No one is safe. This man needs to be stopped before he gets his hands on some real weapons of mass destruction, like nuclear or chemical, and hands them over to the Venezuelan government, or one that's even more unstable and ready to launch an attack on the United States. He's breaking every international law concerning arms sales, but the United States can't touch him. He's a menace to the world and the government in Venezuela protects him. They seem to have no intention of stopping him. They know he's on our target list and I think they protect him just to piss us off."

Relations between the United States and Venezuela were pretty bad and getting worse. Don knew that much. The Venezuelan president blamed the United States for his country's problems, using the U.S. as a scapegoat to keep the focus of his people off his own leadership failures. As long as the people had someone else to hate and fear, he could continue to ravage the country for his own personal gain, all the time portraying himself as doing everything humanly capable to help the poor people living in the slums with no clean water, good food, or jobs. He was being portrayed in the media of the U.S. as an unpredictable, paranoid dictator who had it out for the United States. Most would agree this portrayal, while maybe biased, was certainly more accurate.

"This is big. How the hell are we supposed to take this guy out?" asked Don

"It's not going to be easy, but we've got a plan." Peter assured the group.

"His complex is just outside of Caracas in a small town called Santa Rosa. His security is top notch and highly trained, and he never travels without bodyguards around him. Kroslak employs about a hundred people at his ranch. Most of them are farmworkers who take care of the 5,000 acres surrounding his complex. He has another twenty or so employees in his business offices. These twenty are accountants, secretaries, scientists, communication personnel, and other business experts needed to keep his criminal dealings around the globe running smoothly. You will see in the photos his private jet, a Blackhawk helicopter, and the satellite dishes at the main operations building. He can get out of there at a moment's notice, so we have to keep him from suspecting anything."

One of the suits finally spoke up. Don was convinced he was with the CIA.

"There is a Catholic church in the small village near the ranch. Kroslak supports the church because most of his employees are Catholic and it keeps things simple for him, makes him look good in the eyes of the people. A Father Cabanas runs the church and according to our sources has access to the ranch at any time. Kroslak trusts him and it appears Cabanas has no idea what Kroslak really does, at least that he lets on. He probably knows he's got it good, so he doesn't make any waves. Look at his photo well Don. The plan is for you to go undercover as a priest to Cabanas' church."

Don couldn't hold back his chuckle. "A priest? Now that's a bad plan," he said, only half joking.

CAL BYERS AND WENDY BRUNNER

"I know what you're thinking, but just hear me out," Peter continued.

"We have contacts in Cuba where you'll go for a few days for training as a priest. You're going to be low-key; you're on sabbatical so you won't be expected to do much. You'll really just have to learn the demeanor and when you're with Cabanas avoid theological discussions."

"That shouldn't be a problem." Don couldn't help his sarcasm.

"Your path will be untraceable and there are no hassles getting to Venezuela from Cuba. You will then go to Caracas and we have arranged for you to travel to Santa Rosa. You will have proper paperwork, from no less than the Vatican itself, that you are there on a sabbatical visit on your way to Chile. You will be seen as a priestly VIP, being sent on a very important mission, with the lovely little village of Santa Rosa as your resting stop before beginning your labors. Oh, and your undercover name is Father James."

"Father Cabanas is not to know anything else about you. He is a strong supporter of Kroslak, and Kroslak of his church. Again, they are tied at the hip, and either the good Father doesn't know who Kroslak really is, or he doesn't care, because he knows not to look a gift horse in the mouth. You and Bob are going to do the hit, but you won't see each other until then. Once you're settled in at the church, Manny here will deliver the van with several packages in it that will have everything Bob will need, detonation cords, blasting caps, and electrical detonation devices with blocks of C-4 charges, a gun, radio, maps, and a knife. Manny will also handle the exit strategy from a nearby airfield. Bob will be nearby at all times, keeping low, ready to move."

"The idea is, you'll gain access to the complex with Father Cabanas, figure out the flow of the compound and what's going on, and then determine the exact time and place for when the hit is to occur. The tricky part will be getting back into the ranch, past the armed guards with Bob, probably hiding in the back of the van. Using your own surveillance and the sat images in your folder, you'll have to be able to direct Bob exactly where to go to lay the charges. Then, he'll set the C-4 charges at the prime locations while you deal with Kroslak the best way you see fit. Of course, all of this is subject to change. Once you get there, the final plan is up to you, based on what you learn on the ground, but we thought we'd give you the idea since this is a pretty complicated mission. The good news, or maybe the bad news, I don't know, is by the time you get all this in place it will nearly be Christmas. The plan is to give these guys one hell of a Christmas party."

"Priority one of course is for Manny to secure the escape out of Venezuela. Priority two is for Don to kill Kroslak using whatever means is available. And priority three is for Bob to take out as much of the compound as possible so they can't start up operations again."

He turned and spoke directly to Don.

"Don, you have been loyal to our cause over the past few years and your services have been invaluable to the security of our country," Peter knew how to lay it on.

"You have the most difficult aspect of this mission, the one with the most uncertainty and risk. If you can eliminate Kroslak, this will be your last mission if you want. We're asking a lot, we know. But, we wouldn't ask if we didn't have confidence in you and the whole team. This mission is much more dangerous than previous work and all of you will be well compensated for this, of course. But Don, if you want out after this, or even now, just let me know. No hard feelings. If you choose to accept this one, you will have to go to Cuba in two weeks. Then, you'll be gone for at least two weeks. Take some time to think about it, but you'll have to decide pretty fast to get this moving. If you're on board, you'll have to find a way to let your employer and your family know that you will be gone for a while at Christmas too."

That was it.

They left, and as usual went their separate ways, each to think about what they would do. Don knew the payout would be good. He knew this guy was a top world player in the drug trade, and taking him out would make him feel like he made a big difference in making life harder for these guys.

He knew he'd go. But what was he going to tell Diana this time? It would sure have to be good.

Chapter 11
CUBA

THE STORY WENT something like this. Con Air was having a major push at the end of the year and he was chosen to supervise the transfers of hundreds of prisoners and illegals over the next couple of weeks. He would be flying around, not based anywhere and it would be hard to communicate with him, especially while he was in some foreign country. He would act like he didn't really want to do it, but that the money would be great and he would assure her he would be home by Christmas. She wasn't too happy about it when he told her, but she also knew she wasn't going to talk him out of it.

Don's instructions were to fly to Nassau in the Bahamas. This was the typical work-around for the United States' ban on travel to the island of Cuba. There he boarded a Russian built Aeroflot prop plane to Cuba. It was close to Christmas vacation and the plane was packed with revelers from all over the world. Aeroflot wasn't known for its on-time performance, and they sat on the tarmac while the cabin became a sauna thanks to the strong Bahamian sun. The two flight attendants began pushing their carts up and down the aisle, selling Coke, liquor, snacks and Cuban made trinkets to keep everyone busy. Don took a look out his window at the oil dripping out of the massive engines and thought, "What the hell, I'd better have a drink." He thought he'd get into the Cuban spirit with a bottle of rum and a Coke.

At the airport in Havana, Cuba he sweated a bit through the usual customs and immigration checks. At this point he was just a tourist and he rattled off the name of a hotel by the beach where he said he was headed. They did a pretty thorough search of his bag, and he was glad all the paperwork and anything else he needed would be delivered to him. To customs, he was just another tourist. Finding nothing suspicious, the officer stamped a small piece of paper and inserted it into his passport.

Outside, it was about the same temperature as Arizona, about seventy-five degrees. It was humid though, and it looked like a storm was brewing for the afternoon. Typical tropical weather.

He spotted a man wearing a white straw hat holding up a sign with the words "D Juan" inked out on the cardboard. That was his cue.

Approaching the man, he said, "I'm Don, are you here for me?"

"Si, Si, Si Señor. You're Don Juan? Welcome to Cuba. My taxi is right over there," he said, pointing to a red fifty-seven Packard.

Don couldn't remember ever seeing a Packard that old and in such great shape. This was going to be one heck of a trip. They didn't even make it into Havana. The taxi driver took Don to a small motel just a few miles away from the airport and dropped him off. He had said in broken English that someone would be by the following morning to see him. So, Don settled into the worn out room, complete with sagging mattress, rusty bathroom, and no air conditioning. It wasn't too hot but the air conditioner might have helped with the humidity and the smell. It smelled of Clorox bleach, which he guessed meant it was clean. He was glad he had brought the bottle of rum he'd bought on the plane. It was going to be one of those nights. Best to kick back with the bottle, tune out to the sound of the TV he couldn't understand and just get through the night. Too much thinking about where he was or what he was doing wouldn't do any good. He just needed to plow ahead. The plan was in motion, and though he could have bailed if he really wanted to, he wouldn't. Call it bravado, pride, or just plain stupidity; he was in it now until the conclusion. Whatever that might be.

At first light he startled to a sharp knock at the door. With only his boxers on, he cautiously cracked the door to see a new contact standing there. Behind the guy, he spotted a bright yellow Volkswagen Beetle, another blast from the past, still in great shape.

"Buenos dias, Señor. I am Hugo Vargas. I am here to get you on your way. We should leave as soon as possible, when you are ready. Please quickly sir."

Don did as he was told, and minutes later found himself in the VW bouncing down the potholed roads and along the sea to downtown Havana.

"Did you sleep well, my friend?" Hugo asked.

"Not really," Don said, still a little hung over from the rum. "I could use a cup of coffee."

"Ah yes, no problemo. We'll stop on the way. My sister has a little restaurant and she is a very good cook."

Don sized up Hugo. He wasn't a real big player in this drama that was about to unfold in Venezuela, but obviously he had some connections here in Cuba. Not that Don wanted to know the details but he liked to understand who he was dealing with.

"So Hugo, what's the plan here? I'm a little in the dark about what is to happen today." Don started probing.

"Yes. My instructions are that after we have breakfast, I am to take you to the Catholic mission house where you'll be staying two days. Then, on the third day I am to pick up your new passport and plane ticket out of here. I will deliver them to you and bring you back to the airport. That is all I know my friend."

Well, good enough for now Don thought, phase one was underway. But, a Catholic mission for two days. This would be interesting. He still had some rum at least.

On their way into town, the scenery transfixed Don. They passed rows and rows of dilapidated mansions. Cuba had once been a jewel in the Caribbean. The explosion in growth of the sugar industry and investment from the United States helped Havana to become a city with lots of money and style. It was even called the Paris of the Caribbean.

In the 1950s, it was the place to go for gambling and partying. It was easy to get to, just off the coast of Florida and people flocked to Havana for all kinds of fun, both innocent and not so innocent. Of course, all of the wealth heading to

Cuba attracted the underground. The Mafia was big and in control of much of the money that flowed to and from the island. During Havana's heyday, the rich, famous, and powerful lined the boulevards with mansions, each grander than the next. Royalty, movie stars, business tycoons, and Mafia bosses displayed their wealth and success with elaborate, gated homes along the palm-lined avenues and boulevards.

But now, and for the past few decades, things were different in Havana. These once magnificent homes had fallen into disrepair as the people and their money left with the rise of Communism. Now, the mansions of the elite were merely buildings and places for destitute families to find refuge and put a roof over their heads. The once lavish gardens and pools had no rich owners lounging away the day in them and were now neglected and falling apart. The twenty-, thirty-, or even forty-room mansions housed hundreds of people as makeshift apartment buildings. Havana appeared to be a worn out city in need of everything. After a while, Don couldn't look anymore and stared ahead as they drove along the coast road with upscale hotels on the ocean's edge. These days the hotels were filled with tourists from Europe, Canada, South America, and of course the United States. Everyone knew how to get around the U.S. travel ban to the island, and United States Customs and Immigration wasn't giving anyone a hard time about it anymore. They had bigger things to worry about than who was getting a suntan and drinking rum cokes in Havana.

They drove deeper into downtown Havana, heading for the restaurant of Hugo's sister. Don noticed armed Cuban policemen posted at many intersections, with Uzis strapped around their shoulders. Dressed in camouflaged uniforms with red berets, they were intimidating. It was pretty obvious the military was in control under Fidel and Raul Castro's rule. It made Don uncomfortable to see an Uzi on every corner, but Hugo didn't seem affected by the heavily armed police presence. The police stopped them and Hugo spoke to them in rapid Spanish. The cop was all business and looked over at Don several times during the conversation. Don began to get uncomfortable, but they waved him through. Winding his way through the narrow cobblestone and brick streets in Old Town, Hugo pulled into an alleyway and stopped.

"Here we are. My sister's restaurant," he announced.

They entered using the back door. Inside the steamy café kitchen, they sat down at a table against a back wall, in full view of the small kitchen. A short stocky woman who Don assumed was Hugo's sister placed two cups of cappuccino on the table without looking at them. Don didn't like the atmosphere here. He suddenly felt trapped in the back alley streets of this city, with little information and a known military regime in control. He began to get anxious.

"Listen, my friend," he started. "I don't know who you are or what the fuck we're doing here. How do I know you're not turning me into the authorities?"

"Calm down. It's OK. Cuba is a very dangerous place politically, but you're in good hands with me. I work for your government. Not all of us support the Castro regime. The police and informants are everywhere that is why we are staying low. While you're here the best thing to do is say as little as you can and lie if you say anything. In a police state such as this, a slip of the tongue could land you in prison or worse. Trust no one here. Just listen to me."

The paunchy sister returned and placed two plates on the table, filled with egg omelets smothered in a red spicy salsa. Don was not a fan of spicy food, but beggars couldn't be choosers. He picked around and asked for more coffee. When they finished, Hugo rose and graciously thanked his sister. Don saw him slip a wad of pesos into her apron pocket.

They headed out of the city and to the rolling countryside. With Havana behind them, Don started to relax a bit. The St. Gabriel by the Sea mission complex sat on a bluff overlooking the Caribbean Sea. Don supposed if he had to try to be a priest, at least he would have a great view.

The Catholic Church was loosely tolerated by the regime these days, and it was taking advantage of this by expanding its role in the communities. The church was attracting many of the poor and desperate population who were ignored by the corrupt and badly organized government agencies. The Catholic Church had once been banned completely by the government, which did not even recognize Christmas. Their stance was becoming less restrictive, if for no other reason than the church had the power to keep the people from revolting. Don supposed this was a good place to be. It was under the radar and no one would be asking any questions about what he was doing.

What he was doing was learning how to act like a priest. It would be a quick study of a profession that required lifelong devotion and commitment, but all he had to do was be believable and hope he was never asked to actually take on priestly responsibilities. Hugo pulled off the main road and drove down the dirt road towards the few buildings on the cliff overlooking the sea. He drove around the back and an aging priest met them at the back door to the chapel.

"Hola. I am Father Fausto." The priest shook Don's hand.

Inside he instructed Don to put on a black suit and white collar. Don was getting anxious again. This kind of mission was not like any other, but he kept his cool and did what he was told, all the time hyper-aware of everything going on around him, where he was and his best path of escape.

Hugo slipped out the door and Don heard the VW leaving.

"You must not mingle with the others here at the mission." Father Fausto said.

No problem, Don thought.

"I have a small room for you down the hall and I will bring you your meals there. You will be able to walk about outside, but only towards the east please, so as not to run into others. We have only two days to cover everything so we will have to start tonight."

"The sooner I can get out of here, the better," Don said, looking at the gloomy walls of the mission. He immediately felt bad for badmouthing the good priest's church, but Father Fausto didn't seem to notice and quietly slipped out, motioning for Don to follow him.

The room was spare, which was to be expected in a monastery. There was a cot with a thin mattress, a heavy blanket and a pillow. A sink in the corner had cold running water and there was a toilet behind a makeshift screen. A desk and chair were under the one window, which faced the sea and helped the ambiance some, and a bare light bulb hung from a long black cord in the middle of the ceiling. Despite its lack of amenities it was actually a little nicer than the hotel the night before. Don didn't need much anyway.

That night Father Fausto came to his room as planned armed with a load of books and papers and began his teachings. Don learned the basic rituals of marriage, last rites, baptism, prayers of the sacrament, communion, and the extreme unction for the sick and dying. Though much of the teachings were in Latin or Spanish, Don got the gist of what was given him and remembered much from his childhood catechism days. He brushed up on his Spanish using a cassette player the Father had given him. He studied the voluminous *Catechism of the Catholic Church* and the *Holy Bible*. At several points he wondered if he had bitten off more than he could chew. Hell, he hadn't been to church in a month of Sundays and now he was supposed to be able to lead a mass.

But, Don learned quickly and by the end of the second day, he felt he could play the role of a priest well enough for the situation he was heading into. He was sure ready to get out of that cave and leave Cuba too. Just as he had said, Hugo came to the mission the morning of the third day to take Don to the airport.

Hugo handed over a new passport stating Don was now Father James. There were also a bunch of documents that looked like official Vatican documents talking about Father James' transfer to Chile and sabbatical in Venezuela. Don was impressed with the thoroughness, and it helped him breathe easier. Maybe he was going to get out of Cuba without a hassle. Then Hugo handed Don a one-way ticket to Caracas, Venezuela.

"Good luck, my friend. I hope we meet again."

Not likely Don thought, but "Gracias, Hugo" was all he said.

Chapter 12
FATHER JAMES

WHEN HE LANDED in Venezuela Don grabbed a cab at the airport and was driven to the bus station in a run-down section of the bustling capital city of Caracas. His instructions, given to him by Hugo, had him taking the bus to the little town where Kroslak ran his operation from. A bus, Don thought, this was not going to be fun. He supposed as a humble priest he wasn't supposed to travel first class though. At the station, he boarded a rickety school bus bound for Santa Rosa where he hoped to find the Holy Covenant church. He found a seat in the back of the crowded, bright yellow, graffiti-adorned bus. There were no shocks to speak of so they bounced along the roads, which were in desperate need of a little maintenance. Now and then the main road would turn to dirt in places where it had been diverted around washouts.

People got on and off at every stop, but the bus remained full. For a while, his seat was between a farmer holding a chicken under his arm on one side, and a fat lady loaded with shopping bags on the other side. This wasn't the express route and the trip seemed to take forever with stops in every little village along the way. Nodding off occasionally, Don had no idea what lay ahead for him. He tried not to think too far ahead just yet, but he was anxious to get there and see what kind of plan he could devise to eliminate Kroslak. He sure hoped he hadn't signed on to a suicide mission in this remote part of the world. He avoided thinking about his family.

Santa Rosa was the end of the line. There was a small station and some people waiting around to meet passengers. Don used his broken Spanish to hire a cab to take him to the church. The driver knew where it was, or so he said. It was a few miles outside of town, Don knew this much from the photos he had seen back at the briefing. He finally arrived at midnight in a rainstorm and the cab dropped him off at the chapel. He sought shelter under a portico leading into the chapel. Surveying his surroundings, he spotted a light in a small house beside the church, so he covered his head with his jacket and ran for the light. He knocked on the door and a small rotund man with round gold eyeglasses answered. He was wearing a nightshirt and held a newspaper in his hand.

"Hola. Puedo ayudarte?"

Noticing right away Don was a gringo, he quickly switched to English.

"May I help you?"

For a moment Don had to remember his new name.

"Father James." he said. Don was about to say "I've been traveling for twelve fucking hours and the bus ride and cab ride were a fucking piece of shit. It's raining out here so let me in," but he caught himself before it came out.

"Oh, yes. Yes. Forgive me. I've been expecting you, but I thought it would not be until tomorrow. Come inside. I'm Father Cabanas. How was your trip?"

"Very long and tiring, Father." Don held back, entering the small house.

"Would you like some tea or anything to drink?"

Don really wanted a glass of wine, but dared not ask the good Father, so he said, "No thanks, I'd really just like to dry off and get to bed."

"Si, I'm sure it has been a long journey. You'll be staying in the Parish House. There is a desk and a cot set up for you there. As you see, we are very small and we're not really set up to receive visitors here."

"Thanks for taking me in. I'll try to stay out of your way while I'm here."

Father Cabanas led Don outside and through a garden to the parish house. The small room was not unlike the one in Cuba, but was a bit nicer. The bed was proper and there were a couple of paintings of biblical scenes on the walls. A small window looked out onto the garden.

"I hope this will do for your stay," Father Cabanas said humbly.

"Of course. This is just fine." Don assured him.

"So, I'm expecting a package sometime tomorrow. Some things from home."

"OK. Very good. It will come to my house. Why don't you come to my house tomorrow morning when you awaken and we'll have breakfast? Then I'll show you around the church and get you settled."

"Perfect. I will be there."

"Goodnight then."

Don found himself alone for the first time since leaving Cuba. He was exhausted from the trip and after a quick slug from the bottle of rum he fell asleep as soon as his head hit the pillow. Planning would have to wait another day.

As promised, Father Cabanas fixed breakfast for Don. The Father had a small kitchen with a hotplate and a mini-fridge. Breakfast was coffee, some eggs and fresh corn tortillas. They chatted about the weather, and a little about politics while they ate. After the meal Father Cabanas showed Don around the grounds. They strolled through the chapel, Don acting the part of a fellow priest, talking about the area and the people.

Then Father Cabanas asked, "Why of all places would you decide to take a sabbatical in a place like this?"

"Actually, I'm on my way to Chile to set up a mission house there. This was as good a stopping place as any before I go there. I wanted to spend time in the country and I was hoping to ease into South America and the people, and perhaps learn a thing or two from what you are doing here. I have heard you have a nice community here that provides many services to the people. The community I am heading to is very poor and needs some leadership. I hope I can be of service and help them out." Don lied and hoped his flattery would work its charms.

"Ah, yes. We are doing OK here thanks to a few friends. But, we also have our own problems. We have a lot of poverty, medical problems, and very little schooling for the children. Of course, we get a small allotment from the diocese, which helps some. We get nothing from the government though.

The Venezuelan government is more interested in politics and money to put in its own pockets, than in helping the people who live here in the country. "

"How do you keep things going?" Don began to probe to find out the truth of the situation here.

"We rely mainly on contributions from our generous friends who live in the area." This was just what Don wanted to hear to draw out more information.

"So there are some with money here?" Don ventured.

"A few businessmen and local ranchers. Our main contributor is a very good friend of mine. Señor Kroslak is his name. He has a beautiful ranch about ten miles from here and he is a very kind and good man to the people of Santa Rosa. Without him, I don't know what we would do. He is a very good and generous man."

Don took a moment to digest what Father Cabanas had just said. Father Cabanas was obviously loyal to Kroslak and Don knew he couldn't be trusted. His words were the confirmation he needed. Don would have to play it cool when Kroslak's name was mentioned, yet find out as much as he could. He sure didn't need to tip Cabanas off that he was there to kill Kroslak.

"What kind of ranching does he do?" Don asked, playing dumb.

"Mostly cattle and horses. He is quite a popular figure in this area. If it weren't for Bernard, this church wouldn't exist. He takes a very strong interest in my church and its people, and he is the first to help whenever there is a need."

Don had to grit his teeth to hold back his anger. Evidently, the priest and the people living in Santa Rosa had no idea Kroslak was an international terrorist and cold-blooded killer.

They were walking along the path in front of the house. The weather had cleared and the day was turning out to be sunny and warm. Don was starting to itch in his priest collar. Just then a green dented pickup truck reeking of gas fumes came up the driveway. Stopping beside the two men, the driver said, "I have a delivery for a Father James." He had a strong Spanish accent, but Don immediately recognized Manny Perez as the driver. He wanted to jump up and down for joy at seeing someone familiar and to give Manny a hard time about the accent, but controlled himself. Manny didn't even look at Don, which was a good thing.

"I'm Father James," Don said smiling ever so slightly at Manny.

Manny passed the box to Don, nodded, and drove away.

Eyeing the exchange Father Cabanas seemed to get more curious, "It's strange to get a package delivered out this far in the country. Is it something from home?"

"Oh, just some medicine for my allergies and some books," Don lied again.

"Anything medically serious?"

"No, just Benadryl for bee stings and fire ants."

"Ah, we have bees and ants everywhere in this country. Be careful where you walk." Father Cabanas seemed to drop his questioning.

As they headed back towards the parish house, Don thought he'd move things along a bit further.

"Oh, by the way Father Cabanas, I have rented a van for the short time I'll be here. It will help me to get out and see the people. They told me in Caracas that it would be delivered by noon."

Father Cabanas looked sideways at Don, "My goodness you are resourceful. Transportation in these parts is a real luxury. When it arrives maybe we can take a drive around the countryside together. You can meet some of our parishioners if you'd like." Don was worried that Father Cabanas was becoming more suspicious of his visitor.

"Yes, I'd like that." Don answered trying to sound eager.

Don returned to the parish house and quickly opened the box. Inside he found a disposable cell phone, detailed maps of the area, a Glock handgun, binoculars, a knife, and a packet containing two cyanide tablets. That was pretty sobering, but he reasoned Manny had added the cyanide for him and Bob should they be captured. At the bottom of the box, Don found three half-pound packs of C-4 plastic explosive and charges with timing devices. This was serious stuff. Bob Kiser would use the C-4 later if Don could smuggle him into Kroslak's ranch.

C-4 was one of the best, and one of the worst, weapons available. It had the consistency of modeling clay, so you could form it into any shape you needed and even control the direction of the explosion with it. It was very stable. It wouldn't explode spontaneously. You could drop it, fire a gun at it or even set it on fire and nothing would happen. To explode, it needed a combination of extreme heat and a shockwave. That's what the detonators were for.

Don sat down. He was becoming more and more shocked by the complexity of the mission. He understood now why Peter had given him the option to back out. This was big and required careful planning if he was going to get he and Bob out alive.

He decided he needed much more information and he would have to take a "wait and see" attitude about whether killing Kroslak could actually be accomplished. Acting as a priest, he had to get inside the ranch complex and look at the possibilities. If it appeared to be too dangerous he would pull the plug on the whole operation and get out of Venezuela quickly. He had accomplished every other mission they had sent him on, but this one not only required him to kill Kroslak, but also to destroy his complex. And, he had the distinct feeling all outsiders were automatically suspicious to everyone around here.

Chapter 13
VENEZUELA

JUST AS PLANNED, at noon the next day a white van pulled into the church driveway. Don, as Father James, was there to meet it. Don figured Father Cabanas was probably watching from the window of his house so he played it cool when he saw Bob behind the wheel. The pieces were all in place. Manny was here. Bob was here, and now the van had arrived. Don and Bob were careful not to arouse suspicion. They didn't even shake hands.

"We all set?" Bob queried quietly.

"We're getting there. This shit is crazy and I'm not sure it's going to happen yet," Don murmured. "I'm going to try to get to that ranch today. The good Father and I will go on a little tour in our hot rod here."

"OK, keep me posted. I'm nearby." And with that, Bob turned and got into a car that had followed the van. Manny was behind the wheel and his two partners drove away leaving him to figure out the rest of this mission and how to get them all out alive.

Father Cabanas' curiosity got the better of him so he

came outside to talk to Father James.

"This is a very nice van you have rented."

"Yes, I'd like to see more of the countryside while I'm here," Don said, knowing what he really meant was he now had the means to move closer to this target and eventually to escape.

"I can show you around the area if you'd like, there is much to see here." Cabanas said.

"Sure, that would be nice if you could spare the time."

"Of course, let me just turn off my radio and we will take a little drive."

This was perfect Don thought. He was growing antsy just hanging around a church with the lurking Father Cabanas. All he could think of was the plan, how he was going to get things in to motion quickly and how he'd get out with his team intact. He was anxious to get to the ranch, to gain access and to meet this asshole Kroslak. If this plan was going anywhere, it meant Don had lots of reconnaissance and planning to do and the only way to do it right was to have direct access to the target.

With Don behind the wheel, the two of them drove off into the tropical countryside. Venezuela really was a beautiful country. It was too bad crooks, thugs, and drug dealers ran it. The people didn't deserve to get so little from their government, while the fat cats lived the good life. From what he had seen on his long trip from Caracas, the people were friendly, hardworking, and generous. Coming to places like this made Don even more proud to be an American. Despite its problems, his government was still something to be proud of, and to fight for. As far as he could tell, governments in places like this should be taken out just like the drug dealers and criminals they worked for.

Don pushed the van to its limits on the pothole-filled dirt roads of Santa Rosa. Cabanas waved at passersby walking or on horseback, as Don took note of everything he was saying, listening for clues and bits of information that would help. They stopped for lunch at a little shack on the side of the main road into town. The owner was a little old lady with deeply grooved, darkly tanned skin and just a few teeth left. She was obviously honored to have Father Cabanas in her restaurant, and she bowed and genuflected them all the way to her best table. They got the royal treatment, rice, beans, marinated pork, and even beer. Don actually relaxed and enjoyed his holy lunch with Father Cabanas. He probed, trying to find out more about the priest, but Father Cabanas talked only of his parishioners and his work with them. He didn't give anything away to make Don suspicious he was involved with Kroslak's work, or that he even knew about it for that matter. Even when Don casually brought up what he had heard about people hiding out in the mountains here, Father Cabanas acknowledged nothing. He had no tell, gave nothing away. Either he was really good, or he was really innocent.

The woman would not accept payment from the two priests, but on their way out Don stuffed some pesos under his plate for her. Father Cabanas said he would send some supplies over later with a messenger. His people were proud, he explained. They headed to the other side of the valley and after a while Don put his ulterior motive into action and headed towards Kroslak's ranch; trying to remember the general location from the maps he had studied.

Soon they came upon a wide expanse of cleared fields, meadows, and several buildings could be seen in the valley a little below. With a couple of beers in him, Don was feeling pretty good and the scenery was beautiful.

"Is that a ranch?" Don asked, knowing full well whose ranch it was, but playing the role of the innocent.

"Yes, that is Rancho de Valle," Cabanas said, rather proudly. He even seemed to sit up a little taller in his seat as the ranch came into better view.

"It's the biggest and nicest ranch in this area and is owned by my good friend, Bernard Kroslak. Would you like to see it? I can go there anytime."

"Yes, I'd like that." Don hid his enthusiasm and nervousness about finally being so close to the target. This was just the opportunity he was trying to create. All along he knew he needed to get into that ranch to make his plan, but was both surprised and relieved he had made it happen so easily.

He wheeled onto the road leading to the ranch, taking in every detail. The road was quiet, which was good. Soon, they saw the gate on the right hand side. Kroslak was not hiding anything here. A twenty-five foot high arched gate restricted access to the driveway. For Don, what gave the operation away was the guard shack. It was no shack. It was obviously heavily reinforced to resist attack, with bulletproof and smoked glass and it was probably loaded with serious weapons. Elaborately written across the top of the gate arch was the name of the ranch, "Rancho de Valle" forged in metal. There was no mistake about where they were. They approached the guardhouse and two armed guards wielding M-16 assault rifles stopped them. Don took a silent deep breath and rolled down the window.

"Buenos Dias" the guard said as he leaned in the open window. The guard looked at Don and then at Father Cabanas, who the guard recognized immediately. Don was thankful he was wearing his collar. Hopefully, all his priestly training was not for nothing.

"Ah, Padre. Cómo está?" Father Cabanas and the guard exchanged a few words in Spanish and then the van was waved through the gate. Under any other circumstances, the guards would have denied them, or worse, but the priests were welcome anytime and a friend of Father Cabanas was obviously above suspicion. Don felt a renewed confidence.

"Why all the security?" Don played dumb hoping to get more information, as he started down the long and gently winding driveway that Don presumed led to the main house.

"Security here is important. There are bandits and thieves in the hills who rob travelers on the roads and sometimes in their homes. It's just a precaution."

Like hell, Don thought. He knew damn well what was going on at the ranch and it sure as hell wasn't all ranching. The tree-lined road was bucolic, but as they rounded the final corner, the large satellite dishes and antennas surrounding the main house suggested something else was going on. Father Cabanas was unaware, or more likely just didn't care, what his terrorist friend Kroslak was doing. Don still wasn't sure if Father Cabanas was complicit or ignorant.

Near the main house, another armed guard directed the van to a parking space. The two priests got out of the van and were greeted by a welcoming committee; two attractive twenty-year-old girls dressed in skimpy bikinis with sheer cover-ups. They were on their way for a swim in the Olympic-sized pool by the gardens.

"Hello, Father Cabanas," they called out in unison, as they hurried towards him and gave him a big hug.

"Father James, this is Francesca and Dortea. They are guests of Mr. Kroslak and sometimes attend our services at the church. Don thought, these two whores really needed a little religion in their lives. They giggled as they eyed Don and he knew they had no respect for the collar. He guessed anything was fair game in a place like this. These people had their own rules.

"Where is Bernard, my dears?"

"He is riding his new Appaloosa by the lake."

"We'll find him," Father Cabanas said, turning to leave the two giggling girls. They had taken a definite liking to Don. He must have had the scent of the new guy and no doubt they must have found him very handsome in his priest attire. They shot him a parting glance as they giggled their way down towards the pool. Don and Father Cabanas headed towards the massive barn. Don took note of several buildings and high-end cars. Off a ways, he could see what was probably a hangar and beyond that a large open area that Don guessed was the airstrip. He noticed a few men, all in blue shirts and dark pants, likely the security uniform. Everyone had a weapon and it was always clearly visible.

They walked past the barn and saw two horseback riders galloping at full speed up the road. Don tensed. He sensed he was about to meet his target. The horses reared back as the riders stopped beside the two priests.

"Well, Father Cabanas, what brings you out this way?"

the middle aged, bleach blonde Kroslak said, smiling broadly. He was exactly as Don had pictured him from the photos he'd seen at the training session in Phoenix. He tried not to let the hatred he felt for this man show.

"Just showing Father James around the area." He introduced Don to Bernard Kroslak who reached down from his horse and shook Don's hand. It took a great deal of willpower for Don not to drag him off the horse and choke him to death right there. But, that would have been suicide too. Kroslak's time would come and not soon enough for Don.

"Father James is on a sabbatical at my church for a few weeks."

"Welcome Father James," Kroslak met Don's eyes, sizing him up. Don met his match, not willing to show any sign of weakness to this prick, even if it caused him trouble. Don put on his best smile as he threw daggers through his eyes.

On the other horse beside Kroslak's was a dark man with what seemed to be a permanent scowl on his face. His black steely eyes could send cold chills up your spine. He stared at Don intently, sizing him up.

Cabanas said, "Richardo there is head of security here at the ranch. Why haven't you been to church lately, Richardo?" The scowl on Richardo's face became more intense, but he didn't reply or shift his eyes from staring at Don.

"I don't think Richardo is a good candidate for the Lord," Kroslak answered for him, laughing out loud and slapping the scowling Richardo's shoulder.

"Would you gentlemen like a drink?"

"No gracias. We just stopped by to say hello to you and a few of the parishioners. As you know, half of your employees are members of my church and they are good people. They attend regularly, as all good Catholics should," Father Cabanas was not subtle. He may or may not have been involved with Kroslak's operation, but it was clear he was first and foremost a man of the cloth. "I like to drop in on them now and then to keep them coming."

"Whatever makes them happy, right Father?" Kroslak laughed.

"We hope to see you both at mass Sunday; it is the holy season you know. By the way Bernard, our annual fundraising effort is just underway. I just wanted to let you know we are always in need of donations and support for our church."

Kroslak chuckled aloud, "Of course Father. I'll send over a donation right away."

"Make sure you and Father James stop by for a Christmas drink at the house," he added.

With that, he whipped his horse and they rode away. His ugly face would stay imprinted on Don's mind until the day they met one on one.

Leaving the complex Don made mental notes on the layout of the grounds. He noted one building in particular was surrounded with ten foot razor wire fencing. Based on the electronics, Don knew this was the communications building and one of their prime targets. If they could destroy this building and all the high-tech communications equipment in it no one, including Kroslak, should he by some slim chance live through the attack, would be able to continue the operations. Don needed to give Bob as much information as he could so the C-4 could be quickly placed to do maximum destruction. There were armed guards posted at the doors of the communication building, but there was a clear path behind the building that led from the main house. A Lamborghini and a high performance Ferrari were parked outside of the adjoining garage along with a midnight black Chrysler 300 rolling on chrome dubs. Don just shook his head. There were hundreds of thousands of dollars just in cars sitting right in front of him. And, those were the least valuable of Kroslak's possessions. Needless to say, video cameras were installed on posts everywhere, surveying every inch of the grounds. To destroy these structures was not going to be an easy job for Bob Kiser, and Don knew they would have to do it under the cover of night to avoid the cameras.

On the way out to the entry gate, they took a side road and passed the helicopter sitting next to the runway where a Citation jet sat ready to go at any time. The spoils of the drug war had been good to Kroslak. All this decadence and excessive wealth made Don more determined than ever to complete this mission. Especially after he had seen the good people of the village and what very little they had. Don thought about Bernard Kroslak and how he was instrumental in helping the killers and drug dealers of this world prey on innocent people. He thought about the amount of drugs this guy pushed through to the streets of the U.S. and of the young people and their families whose lives were ruined because getting access to Kroslak's drugs was so easy. He thought about the smirk on Kroslak's ugly mug and the attitude he portrayed that he could do anything he wanted, at any time, to anyone. All he needed, and had, was money. The man was a megalomaniac, drunk on his own delusion of power and control. It was time to stop him.

Chapter 14
THE PLAN

IT WAS THE week before Christmas. Don lay on his cot at the mission house thinking about how he could get his hands on Kroslak. He was anxious to get this mission over with so he could get back and spend time with his family over the holidays, but it was important not to rush. This was a tricky job, dealing with high-stakes players.

Rancho de Valle seemed impenetrable. Any approach, especially during daylight hours, would be extremely risky with all the security guards, cameras, and electrified fences. He wasn't sure of what exactly was in the buildings surrounding the house, but at the training session in Phoenix Peter had made it quite clear they needed to be destroyed. They were even instructed to destroy the jet and the helicopter.

He had only four C-4 charges and timers for Bob Kiser to plant so they would have to be placed wisely, for maximum effect. However, before any of that could happen Don needed to get into the ranch. How to do this was the big question. The guards at the gate clearly recognized and trusted Father Cabanas and had seen Don in the van with him. They had flagged them through without question so Don thought it was possible, since Christmas was so near, that he could enter the complex alone, saying he was on church business. There were plenty of reasons to visit Kroslak or the people who worked on the ranch around Christmas time. And besides, everyone lightened up at the holidays. Don was pretty good at getting people to lighten up, even if they didn't speak English. Dirty jokes worked in pretty much any language. He would just turn on the charm at the gate if he had to. The hard part was finding an excuse to get into the ranch alone. He had to get away from Cabanas for a little while, and with a good reason to go to the ranch in case Cabanas heard about it later.

The hard part was somehow he would have to conceal Bob Kiser in the back of the van. Don could pick him up along the road somewhere, but there was no real good way to hide him in the back of the empty van. They would at least need a blanket for Bob to hide under. They would have to hope the guards would have no reason to take a look in the back, at least a close look. If they did, all hell would have to break loose right then and there at the guard shack and then it would likely be impossible to get at Kroslak. But, if they were prepared to take out the guards at the gate quickly and quietly, they might be able to salvage the mission and get to Kroslak before any of the other security were alerted. It would be risky and if something went wrong at the gate, they would have to decide at the moment whether or not to abandon the mission's objective to take out Kroslak. For now, Don just had to hope there would be no reason to open the back of the van and have a look around.

Once he was in the gate, he needed a plan to be able to find Kroslak and isolate him from his cronies, or the women likely surrounding him. He might just have to wing that part, depending on what was going on when he arrived. But, when a priest asks for a private consultation, it was likely that Kroslak wouldn't say no.

Just then the whine of a small jet roared overhead. Looking out of his window to the sky he recognized the Citation jet from Rancho de Valle. Kroslak was on the move again. The jet banked north and was out of sight within minutes. Don started to get frustrated. Where was he heading? Was he going to leave and foul up the mission?

He was going crazy trying to figure out this big plan in the small church room. He had a lot to think about so he took a walk down the road to clear his mind. There was a small pond down the road, and Don sat there a while throwing rocks in like a kid. The kerplunk sound never failed to satisfy him. The day was heating up again and Don was getting hungry so he headed back to the church, feeling a little calmer. Father Cabanas spotted Don walking back towards the church. He scuffled out and met Don on the road.

"Getting some fresh air?" Don always felt Father Cabanas were testing him. Maybe it was just his own paranoia about being found out, but there was something about Father Cabanas that made Don uneasy.

"Oh sure, I heard a low flying jet before and came out to see it." Don started fishing for information.

"Oh yes. It's from the ranch. Bernard flies in and out on ranch business from time to time. He is a very busy man and has meetings with very important people. Sometimes even with the President."

Don could sense Cabanas knew nothing of Kroslak's dirty dealings around the world. He could sense his reverence for the scumbag.

They walked back towards the house and the rotund priest pulled a sheet of paper out of his pocket.

"I wanted to discuss something with you."

Don got nervous immediately. It sounded official. Was he going to have to perform a service or take confessions? He'd absolve everybody, but still he really didn't want to put his priest knowledge to the test.

"Because it is Christmas, we'll be very busy this week at the church and I was hoping you could help me out." Just as Don feared.

"Of course we'll be offering several additional services and events for the people during Holy Week. I've prepared a program for all the events. Take a look," he said, handing the program to Don.

Studying the program Don quickly scanned to see if there were any events that looked easy. Most of it was in Spanish though and he had only a vague idea of what, beyond mass each one was. He steeled himself and responded,

"Sure. What can I do to help?"

"I don't want to impose on you since you are here to rest, but if you feel up to it you can help me get the word out to the community about our services. As you see I have no transportation here except the horse down in the pasture. Since you have the van I was hoping you could take and distribute the program to all the villages in the area. Celebrating the birth of Christ is very important for our parishioners and we want a full house at every service. If you could distribute these, more people will know and will not be able to make excuses for not attending. It would give you the opportunity to get out into the villages a little too and to meet the local people as well as some of the workers at the ranch."

Don's mood suddenly lightened as he was not only off the hook for preaching to the masses, but he sensed Lady Luck had just handed him a solution to his problem of how to get into the ranch alone, without suspicion.

"I'll be glad distribute the programs." Don could have kissed funny little Father Cabanas right then and there. "Just let me know when they're ready and I'll take a little drive through the countryside with them."

"Excellent. Our first event is a community meal in the rectory this Wednesday, and then every day something is going on here. We'll have mass on Christmas day and prayer service that evening. The program will be ready to distribute tomorrow if I can get the old copy machine working properly."

"I'd be happy to help any way I can. Let me know if you want me to take a look at the machine." Don offered.

"Muchas Gracias. I will let you know when they are ready."

With that said, Father Cabanas turned and waddled away back into the rectory. Don smiled at fate and how things sometimes just fell into place. Distributing the flyers was the perfect alibi for entering Rancho de Valle. And, he would be alone, without Father Cabanas. He'd pick up Bob and hide him in the back, and they'd likely get right past the security gate, after handing them a couple of fliers of course and gaining assurances they'd come to mass. He couldn't have prayed for a better plan.

Back in his room he was now ready to draw up a full plan of attack. He used the disposable cell phone, sure that the team had made it untraceable and called Bob Kiser. It was good to hear a friendly voice on the other end. Don told him it had suddenly all fallen into place. They made plans to meet a few miles outside of the ranch just before sunset the next day. They'd go over the details of placing the explosives and taking down Kroslak then, but Don had the plan already formed in his mind. He had mapped out the complex in his mind and felt certain Bob had enough C-4 to take out the communications, the jet, the helicopter, and the main house. That should do it.

He called Manny to let him know that the escape plan and route had to be ready the next night.

This was it. Everyone was on alert for the hit to go down the following day. Despite the problems with Manny back in Colombia, Don had trust and faith in both these guys, and though he was more nervous about the details than on previous missions, he knew Bob and Manny would do whatever had to be done. More importantly, he knew they would do it right.

The only weak point in the plan was Kroslak. Don had no way to know when Kroslak's jet would return. He could only hope it would be in the next twenty-four hours. He wanted this to be over with as soon as possible. If Kroslak was late, it could still work. Don seemed to have the trust of Father Cabanas now, but waiting was torture.

Don was feeling confident about getting into the ranch with Bob now too. He had two reasons to be entering the ranch legitimately. First, was the official church business of distributing the flyers and making holiday rounds. Second, Kroslak had invited him to stop by for a drink. Don was certain he could use a little Catholic guilt on the guards if they began to give him a hard time.

Since Kroslak had invited him up for a drink, Don also felt certain this meant Kroslak would be back soon. He didn't sound like a man who intended to be away for the holidays. For now, all Don could do was watch the sky for the return of the Citation jet and hope Lady Luck had more in store for him and the team. Once he knew Kroslak was back at the ranch, he'd alert Bob, and the team would jump into action and make their move. Don felt the pressure. This was it. He might only have this one chance, and he didn't want to miss the opportunity to end Kroslak's reign of terror. Thankfully, he had a little bit of rum left. A drink would calm his nerves and get him through what was sure to be a long night in his little church room.

The only murky part of the plan was the escape and how to not be killed in the process of closing up this guy's brutal operation. If he took too long to isolate Kroslak, he might get blown up himself. Or, if all hell broke loose for some reason, he and Bob would have to somehow get down that long driveway and out the gate before anyone came after them. This part of the plan was just going to have to be spontaneous. It made him nervous, but he'd come too far to back out now. Everything was in place, and though he did feel ready and pretty confident overall, he also felt very alone. After all, he had made the plan by himself, and Bob and Manny's lives depended on it being the right plan. He hoped he had observed the ranch well during his short visit and that he could give Bob the right information for setting the charges. If he missed even one crucial detail, a guard, a camera, or some other important piece of information, it could mean Bob's life and maybe even his own. But despite the pressure, he had learned in Vietnam he would rather be giving the orders than getting them. There was also the motivation that this could all be over by tomorrow night. He could be well on his way back to his family to enjoy the rest of the Christmas season.

But, none of that was going to help him sleep tonight.

Chapter 15
BANDITOS

THE BENEFIT OF not sleeping was that during the night Don heard Kroslak's jet return to the ranch. OK, he thought, here we go. There was no turning back now, unless he got a bad feeling during the mission. With just an hour or so of sleep, Don rolled out of bed. Everything seemed more quiet than other days. Even the din of the surrounding tropical jungle was muted. This was how it was sometimes before a hit. The world seemed different, as if Don was moving in a dream of his own creation. Maybe it was because of his focus on what he needed to do, or maybe it was his change in perception that helped him to focus. All he knew was today was the day the mission was going down.

He called Bob Kiser to alert him it was a go and to meet the van on the road one mile from the ranch later that day. He called Manny Perez to make sure plans were ready for a plane out of Venezuela and to confirm where they would meet after all the chaos broke out. He and Bob had worked it all out already. Don wondered where those guys were staying in this crazy country.

He showered, shaved, and put on his black suit and priest collar. He didn't know if he'd be returning to the parish house that night, so he packed all of his personal belongings, but he left a few items around to keep the room from looking abandoned. In this business, the smartest way to go was not to trust anyone, even a priest in a tiny town in Venezuela. He wasn't sure about Father Cabanas. His loyalty to Kroslak seemed to run deep, and if he checked Don's room and thought he had abandoned it, who knows what he would do with that information. So Don played it safe and left some toiletries and one of the robes he had been given in Cuba behind. He left a bible opened on the bed, as if he had just been reading it like the good priest he was.

He pulled out the cardboard box Bob Kiser had delivered to him from under the bed. Opening the lid, he found a pair of white gloves and he slipped them on. He then took out the Glock and slid the full clip into it. Inside he found the four C-4 charges with timers Bob Kiser would place in the jet, the helicopter, and the two main buildings. They were to go off in sequence once Don was in contact with the target. He found a flashlight, maps, and a holstered serrated military knife. He noticed the small packet with two cyanide tablets. It reminded him of the seriousness of this mission. Damn, he thought, would he ever take his own life if captured? He was sure Kroslak would kill him if he figured out who Don was or that his boss was the United States government. He was sure Kroslak would kill him no matter what, even if he just figured out Don was not a priest. It's not like Don might be held as a prisoner by Kroslak or the Venezuelan government, one that they could use as a bargaining chip with the

U.S. This was not that kind of game. His own government was not going to bail him out or even acknowledge who he was, if something happened. So just like the other missions, he was acting alone with only his two partners. If they were suspected or caught, the cyanide just might come in handy. These guys would not give him a humane death, of that he was sure. He tucked the pills into the small corner pocket of his jeans and put it out of his mind.

Carefully, he placed everything back into the box and closed the lid. He then took the box out to the van and hid it under the front seat. Returning, he grabbed the blanket off his bed and threw it in the back of the van. The plan was to get Bob in the back of the van and have him hide under the blanket, concealed from the guards at the ranch, and of course hope to hell they had no reason to want to search the van. After a strong cup of coffee and a check of his nerves he wandered outside. As the sun broke through the lush trees surrounding the church, Father Cabanas came outside babbling,

"Good morning my friend. How'd you sleep?"

"Very good," he lied.

"Are you ready to deliver the programs today?"

Don tried not to sound anxious. "Whenever you're ready, I can go this morning."

"I mimeographed the copies last night. They should be dry now. Come in and I'll get you on your way."

Don followed Cabanas into his cluttered three-room house. Entering, he smelled the same combination of incense and wine he'd smelled at breakfast the last he visited. He was more relaxed now than that first day, and he took notice of how the old priest lived. He spotted a well-stocked wine cabinet in the kitchen. This wine was used in the communion services and maybe to help Father Cabanas pass the time. There was a living area with a desk under the window, a small bedroom on one side and an even smaller kitchen in one corner. A thin metal cross, with a crucified Jesus, hung on one wall, a rosary draped around it. Pictures of saints adorned the other walls and a large bible lay open on a stand near the desk. Father Cabanas walked over to the desk, littered with papers, some with official looking seals, and handed Don a stack of the holiday programs.

"This is the best I can do with this antiquated printing equipment."

"They look fine," Don said, still not able to make out much of the Spanish. He took the programs, headed out the door, got into the van and waved goodbye to Cabanas as he drove away. Don felt a little bad. Who knew what would happen to Father Cabanas and his church once Kroslak and his money were gone, that was the only part of this that held a tinge of sadness. But, they had somehow gotten by before Kroslak, and they'd surely do it again. Don knew he'd never see the pudgy priest again and he hoped he wouldn't take the death of his friend too hard, at least not once he found out the truth about him. Don supposed Father Cabanas may never know the truth about Kroslak. If everything went according to plan today, Father Cabanas would never know the truth about Don either.

Don spent a good part of the day doing exactly what Father Cabanas had told him to do. In every village and roadside stand he dropped off programs. For miles he traveled over rough road to get to some of the more remote villages. Everywhere he went he was greeted warmly by the people and he used his meager Spanish to converse and laugh with the locals, and to get directions. He asked for a lunch recommendation in one town and was escorted by one of the men sitting in the square to the best place in town—the patio of his own home. His wife made a home cooked meal, the traditional *pabellón criollo*, or Creole lunch. Don was a meat and potatoes man, but this was the best meal he had had in a couple of weeks. The rice, black beans, fried plantains and a little meat weren't too spicy and just what Don needed to set him up for the rest of this day. His new friend invited him to have a beer but Don had a rule about not drinking when a hit was going down. He needed all of his cylinders firing at peak performance to get this done without losing his life. The drinking would come after it was all over, and then there would be plenty of it.

He had some time to waste because he wanted to pick up Bob Kiser and be at the ranch around sundown. It was just after mid-afternoon and the heat of the day was intense so Don headed the van back towards the ranch. He figured he'd find a nice shady spot for a little quiet time. Like every mission he had been on before, he began to get his mindset into a place where he could visualize what was going to happen, running over the possibilities in his mind. In this case, he was facing the unknown once he got inside the ranch and was face to face with Kroslak. He didn't know if he could pull it off and escape, but he had some ideas.

On a mile long stretch of dirt road, with a canopy of trees forming a tunnel overhead, he spotted a small tree lying across the road in the distance. Standing beside the fallen tree he spotted what looked like two men. A motorcycle was nearby, propped against another tree. One man moved and grabbed the fallen tree and tried to pull it out of the road. Don got immediately suspicious and was on high alert. He casually reached under the seat as he approached and pulled out the military knife and hid it under his shirt. Hanging his head out the window he hollered, "Hey, you need some help?"

"Gracias, if you'd be so kind," one man said. He was wearing a red bandana wrapped around his black, greasy hair. Tattoos ran up and down his arms. His sleeveless t-shirt showed off his muscular biceps. Don could see the letters CAPO were tattooed around his neck. The other man was wearing a leather vest, no shirt and jeans. He was the smaller of the two, but still appeared intimidating. This did not look good, but Don had to pass this road so he had no option but to get out of the van. He walked up to CAPO who was surveying the tree.

"Both of us can grab this end and swing it aside," he said. The smaller man was standing near the motorcycle and didn't offer to help. Don and CAPO budged the tree a little ways when suddenly Don noticed a movement behind him. He turned quickly, but too late and a smashing blow hit him in the back of the head. He was stunned at first and fell to the ground. Through blurry eyes, he watched the two men standing over him. CAPO had a switchblade in his hand and was smiling. Don's senses came back quickly and he knew immediately he was about to become the victim of a roadside robbery. He also knew in Venezuela this didn't just mean they were going to take his van, there was a good chance they were going to kill him.

CAPO leaned down and put the knife to Don's throat. It was a do or die situation. But, Don acted quickly and took CAPO by surprise. He slid his hand behind him, and in one move pulled the military knife out of his belt and jammed the blade into the calf muscle of CAPO. CAPO fell to the ground screaming and writhing. Don scrambled up to his feet just as the other man started towards him. Don kicked him hard in the groin, followed by a crushing upper cut that sent the bandit to the ground. Both guys got up cursing and attacked him from two sides with fists and knives swinging furiously. Don's adrenaline was up now and though there were two of them, they were both smaller than Don and they had no idea how much training Don had had for just this type of situation. Don threw a crushing blow to the smaller man's throat but that didn't stop him. He lunged, his knife aimed at Don, nicking his arm. With blood dripping down his arm, Don stepped back and knew he'd have to put his training to use and kill these guys or be killed.

Viciously, he lunged at CAPO, got him from behind, and with a quick twist of his neck Don heard his vertebrae crack. He immediately fell limply to the ground with a broken neck. The smaller bandit saw he was no match for Don so he ran to the motorcycle and sped off down the road. The little guy's heart was never really in it anyway. Don had taken care of the real threat. CAPO wouldn't be terrorizing motorists any more.

Don dropped to his knees in exhaustion, and in disbelief of what had just happened. He caught his breath, got up, dragged CAPO's body to the side of the road, and rolled him down an embankment. Returning to the van, he took a deep breath and thanked God for his military training in hand-to-hand combat. It had been a while since he had had to use it. It was kind of like riding a bicycle though. Once it started, it flowed on instinct. He wasn't happy about having to do this today, of all days, but in some way it gave him even more confidence and determination to take care of Kroslak. Once he got Kroslak alone, he would be easy to take out compared to those two guys. He wiped the blood from his arm, drove around the tree, which they'd managed to move just enough before Don got jumped, and headed towards the ranch.

He tried to call Bob Kiser on his cell phone but couldn't get reception. He would be picking him up in a couple of hours; that is if he wasn't robbed again in this hellhole of a place. Meanwhile, he'd find a quiet, shaded place to pull over and regroup for the fireworks that were sure to come that night at Rancho de Valle.

Chapter 16
RANCHO DE VALLE

AS LATE AFTERNOON came on, Don drove slowly down the road to the ranch, watching the mileage on the odometer. He knew one mile from the entrance to the ranch, he would find Bob on the side of the road. How he got there was none of Don's concern. Bob could take care of himself and God knows how he managed this one. Knowing him, he was camping out in the woods somewhere eating nuts and berries. Once Bob was in the van with him, they would wait until dark and then try to get past the guards and into the ranch complex.

Sure enough, with one mile to go, there was Bob walking down the road slowly, like a local, wide-brimmed hat and all. Bob pulled up a pant leg and stuck out his bare, white gringo calf to flag the van down. Don couldn't help but laugh at the sight of him. At least something was going right. At least he and Bob hadn't lost their sense of humor. Don drove the van right at him. Don didn't even stop, just slowed it to a crawl. Bob jumped right into the passenger's seat and they kept driving.

"Don't think I'll ever get used to seeing you dressed as a priest!" Bob chided Don.

"Yeah well, don't think you're gonna get something with legs like that. I'm a man of the cloth now anyway."

They both had a good laugh and Bob looked closer at Don, who must have still looked a little unnerved from the day's events.

"What happened to you?" Bob said seeing the gash on Don's arm.

"Oh, not much. Just another day in paradise. I was driving around minding my own priestly business, handing out these flyers. I had a little altercation when I ran into two bandits who blocked the road with a tree and tried to rob me. They probably wanted to take the van, but that wasn't gonna happen. We had a little disagreement. One of them just wouldn't see my side of the story so now he's face down in a ditch. But the other guy knew he was fucked and high-tailed it out of there on a motorcycle."

"Jesus Christ, are you okay?"

"Yeah, but one of the cocksuckers nicked me on the arm with his knife."

"Damn, this fucking place is the arm pit of the world."

"Yeah," Don said, "Even a priest is a target. I bet they thought they had an easy mark when they saw me coming down the road in my little white collar. Bet he'll never mess with a priest again. I may even have made my first convert."

"Well done Father." It looked like the priest disguise would provide them with entertainment for years to come.

"Man, I can't wait to get out of here. Let's get this thing done tonight. "

"You're not gonna get an argument from me," Don said, shifting in his seat.

Bob was ready to get down to business. "So afterwards, Manny has arranged a charter flight out of here at an abandoned airstrip about ten miles from here. We're not hanging around in some hotel after this one, thank God. We do it and we're out as quick as possible. I have a map to find the strip. We have to drive the van directly there after we finish Kroslak off. Manny's got his guys all set up to take care of the rest. Do you have the C-4 charges?"

Don reached under the seat and pulled out the box. Bob examined the timers making little noises of approval. Don supposed that meant it was all OK. It wasn't dark enough yet, so they headed up to the ridge road to get above the ranch. Maybe they could see some goings-on down there while they waited, and Bob could at least get a look at the place before he had to do his work.

"Let's do a little surveillance on the complex. From somewhere up here we should be able to get a better view with the binoculars of the ranch in the valley. You can probably get a better feel for what I told you about the layout," Don said.

They found a well-hidden cart path and backed the van into it, facing the road. It was likely this road up on the ridge was rarely traveled, especially after dark. There were no such things as streetlights in this neck of the jungle, so they got out of the van to stretch and prepare. They walked to the edge of the ridge and Don told Bob again what he had seen on his visit to the complex, about the communications, the jet and the helicopter. Bob took the binoculars and scanned the complex. This was perfect.

Every additional bit of information would help the job to go faster and smoother.

"Okay Don, we're supposed to take out the important buildings, the jet, and the helicopter. From what I see the satellite dishes connect to one big building, obviously a communications building. That will go first. Then all of the charges will go off in a sequence. After the communications building, the jet will go, and then the helicopter and then finally the main house. Once we get in we'll set a time to start the explosions, so let's sync our watches because timing will be crucial. From the first explosion you hear, you will only have about five minutes to get out of the house. If I set them any farther apart it will give the guards time to react and protect. I hope you can get to Kroslak and get out of the house in that time."

"That should be fine. My plan is to go in on church business, delivering programs, and then isolate Kroslak with some lame excuse, maybe about his donation or something. I'll tell him I need a word with him privately just before our agreed time. I have the knife and the Glock on me. I'm not sure which one I'll use. It depends on who else is there and where we are. Hopefully it will be clean and quiet. The less commotion the better. If I can't isolate him in time, I'll just get the hell out and we'll have to hope the explosion takes care of him."

"Are you positive we can get through that entrance gate?" Bob asked.

"Hell, I'm not sure about anything right now. But, the guards know me already as a priest. I came here with Father Cabanas once before and they waved us through. Kroslak invited me for a drink, so I'll just say I'm taking him up on some Christmas cheer or some bullshit. I got a look at those guys at the gate. They're smalltime. A few smiles and a rude joke, especially from the visiting priest, should do the trick."

The sun was setting now, and the surrounding mountains and the valley below were actually quite beautiful. The area was lush with vegetation, and the birds were making a raucous commotion as they settled down for the night. It was good to be out here in nature for a few minutes before the hit went down. It gave Don time to get his mind ready for what was to happen. It was never easy, but he could always stand firm on his reasoning that what guys like Kroslak were doing, without impunity, was wrong. Kroslak was hurting families and ruining the lives of plenty of young people in the U.S. with the drugs he was flooding the streets with. This was a necessary evil of the war on drugs. Men like Kroslak had to go, no matter what, and Don and Bob were the perfect guys to do what others couldn't, or wouldn't.

They returned to the van and waited a little longer. It reminded Don of the many stakeouts he and his partner Harvey had done back in Chicago. Sometimes they'd sit for hours waiting for a subject to appear. Like Bob, Harvey had a way of taking the edge off with his jokes. It was a time on the force Don missed, and it made him wonder how he had ended up here, sitting on the edge of dirt road on a mountain ridge in Venezuela, waiting for the right moment to take out an international criminal. Life sure was unpredictable.

Another thirty minutes passed and the darkness approached rapidly. It was time to get this party going. Don started the van and eased out onto the road. They started down off the ridge and Don could feel the tension rising in his blood as they came closer and closer to the ranch entrance.

When the lights of the gate were in sight Don said,

"Okay, let's get this done. Get into the back and lay flat and cover yourself up with that blanket."

Bob took the C-4 and laid down on the floor close up against the seats, trying to make it look like there was nothing back there at all, should a guard take a look.

Heading down the well-lit ranch driveway, the guardhouse came into view. Don's hands became sweaty, his heartbeat hastened, and he had those feelings he'd had back in Vietnam before a firefight. He stopped the van at the gate. An armed guard came out and up to the window staring at Don in his priest outfit. Don put on his best happy go lucky smile to put the guard at ease.

"Hola Amigo! I'm here to see Mr. Kroslak and deliver these programs for Father Cabanas."

Don showed the guard his fake Father James passport and the programs. He used all his charm, and he was slightly relieved he recognized the guard as the same one he had seen when he and Father Cabanas had come previously. He made some jokes about the guard coming to church, even if just for the wine. And, just for good measure he mentioned how it would be good for his sex life. Women loved men who went to church.

It worked. The guard must have been filled with Christmas cheer and he just smiled and opened the gate, waving the van through. Don breathed a long breath of relief. Step one was conquered. Slowly he drove the van up the long and winding, tree-lined driveway of the ranch, heading closer to his target. He was memorizing the soft turns, anticipating the drive out which would likely be at triple his current speed.

"OK, we're in," he called back to Bob who was still under the blanket.

"Nice work," Bob called up front as he uncovered himself and gathered the tools he needed.

"OK. Let's set our watches for half an hour," Don said. "I don't want to be in there longer than that. That should give me time to schmooze him and take care of him." Is that enough time for you?"

"Yup. It will have to be."

Don had used his previous visit to scope out where to park once he got to the main house. He backed into a space against a hedgerow and far enough from the front door so Bob could exit from the back of the van without anyone seeing him. Music was coming from inside the house and it sounded like a party was in progress. This could be good for Don's plan. If he could isolate Kroslak, the commotion of the party would be a good distraction. Now was the time for Don to become a real "actor."

Bob quietly slipped out the back, leaving the door open just a little for his, hopefully, inevitable return. He scurried off into the darkness to places the charges. Don got out of the van and headed towards the front door, programs in hand. On the grand steps leading up to the entrance another guard, who seemed wholly uninterested in who came and went, just smiled as Don passed. Don tried to put himself in a priestly frame of mind by making a cross in the air in the guard's direction.

"Sorry." Don thought, "Sorry if anything happens to you. You probably have no idea what goes on here. Just a guy trying to make some money."

He couldn't dwell on collateral damage though. Kroslak was in his sights and nothing was going to get in the way of that now. As he stood at the front door of the main house, his focus kicked in to high gear, he took a deep breath and knocked.

Chapter 17
THE HIT

A WELL-DRESSED YOUNG man in a starched white shirt, red bowtie, and black slacks answered the door.

"Hello, I'm Father James. I have something for Mr. Kroslak from the church."

"One moment, please," the teenager replied as he closed the door.

The door swung open moments later and there stood Bernard Kroslak with a big smile on his pocked face. He was wearing a white long sleeved linen shirt with the words Rancho de Valle embroidered in gold on his shirt pocket. With white pajama bottoms and navy bedroom slippers, he appeared very relaxed.

"Come in, come in. To what do we owe this pleasure, Father James I believe it is?"

"Yes sir," Don said entering the foyer. "I have the Christmas programs from the church. Father Cabanas was hoping someone here could distribute them to your employees."

He handed Kroslak a stack of programs, sizing him up as he moved closer. Don was trying to assess how much he'd been drinking and his general attitude and demeanor.

Kroslak quickly looked over the flyers and with a big smile looked up and said, "I'll give them to my foreman. Now, you've come at the perfect time. Come on in and have a holiday drink with us."

Don followed Kroslak into the lavish living room where a fire was blazing in the floor to ceiling stone fireplace, despite the fact it was not nearly cold enough. All the French doors were open out to the patio and the pool and Don thought he even heard the air conditioning running. These guys didn't care about anything except what they wanted. Loud thumping house music blared outside and Don could see a handful of people sitting on chaise loungers, laughing, smoking and drinking. Don hoped they all made it out when the shit went down. Bob had probably already placed the charge. The blast would probably take out the front portion of the main house. He figured they might be injured but as long as they stayed outside they probably wouldn't be killed.

Two men were seated on big leather wing chairs under a dim reading lamp and were in deep conversation. Both men held cocktail glasses and the smaller man was smoking a Cuban cigar.

"Excuse me gentlemen, this is Father James from the Holy Covenant Church. This is Augustine Diaz and this is Mr. Hatcher. They are my guests visiting from Mexico."

Don immediately recognized the name Augustine Diaz from his studies of the Mexican cartels. He was a notorious member of the Las Zetas cartel. He was dressed in a yellow tropical shirt covered with palm trees. He smiled from ear to ear with pearly white teeth, a thin gold chain draped around his pudgy neck. The other guy, Hatcher, had a bald shaved head with steel blue eyes. His bulging muscles stretched his t-shirt to its limits. Judging by the rings and the tattoos, he was evidently Diaz's protection.

"Could I offer you a glass of wine?" Kroslak said politely to Don. "We'll toast in the holidays."

"Thank you, I'll take a little please."

Don had no intention of drinking the wine. He needed to be sharp for the next few minutes, but he knew it would seem odd if he refused. He needed to gain, or keep, the trust of Kroslak if he was to get him alone. Don had the plan formulated in his mind and now was the time to put it into action.

Kroslak turned to the bartender, who was dressed formally and serving from a lavish mirrored bar, which took up one whole side of the large room. He nodded towards the bartender and ordered him to give Don a glass of the best wine he had.

"Come. Let's go out to the pool and you can meet the rest of our little holiday party."

Diaz, Hatcher, and Don followed Kroslak through the French doors. Don glanced at his watch. There were only twenty minutes until Bob would set off the first explosion and all hell would break loose at the ranch. He'd have to work fast to get Kroslak alone.

Before he got a chance, two young topless girls in bikini bottoms grabbed Don as he stepped outside the door and pulled him towards the other partiers. Don recognized the two girls as Francesca and Dortea whom he'd met on the first trip to the ranch. Most of the partygoers were gathered around a small disc jockey's stage now playing very loud merengue music. It looked like Kroslak catered to the young crowd. Maybe he thought of himself as the Venezuelan Hugh Hefner or something. In any other situation, Don might have played along, but he had other things on his mind right now.

The giggling girls hung onto each arm and it was obvious they had drunk plenty of champagne. They were urging Don to get into the heated pool with them. Francesca tried to remove his coat and priest collar. Quickly he stopped her because the Glock was hidden in his back belt under his coat. The knife was inside his coat pocket. Jesus, this was no way to blow the mission.

Kroslak, Diaz, and Hatcher stood to the side laughing as they watched the gregarious girls displaying all the affection towards the timid priest. Several other girls were in the lighted pool along with a number of men in different stages of attire, some nude, some topless, and some even fully dressed. They were all in different stages of drunkenness, or whatever else they were taking to get in the mood. Don was sure they had access to any kind of drug that they wanted. It didn't seem to make any difference to them that a priest had joined their holiday party either. Little did they know what was about to happen to this party. Don was getting anxious. He knew he had to make a move on Kroslak and he had to act fast. He couldn't get rid of the girls politely, who pushed him down on a lounge chair and began dancing seductively in front of him. They obviously didn't care that he was a priest and he wondered if pudgy little Father Cabanas got this treatment. He pretended to enjoy their gyrations for a little while, but his mind and his eyes were on Kroslak. Time was running out.

Finally, having enough and feeling like he'd put on enough of a show, he abruptly got up from the lounger and pushed the girls aside, excusing himself. They seemed dejected at his rejection and hasty departure, but they quickly brushed it off and jumped into the pool with the other guests. In the meantime Diaz and Hatcher had found new company and were enjoying the affections of two young twins. The bartender brought out four glasses of wine to where Kroslak was standing. Don rushed over and took a glass of the wine.

"Just a little harmless fun, eh, Father James?" Diaz said with a smirk on his face.

"Yes, I suppose," Don answered, "but, I must resist temptation in the most holiest of seasons." Don smirked right back.

"So, Father James, where is your church in your home country?" Diaz suddenly seemed interested in Don.

This was the first time Don had been questioned about where he was from, but he was ready.

"My home diocese is in New Jersey, but I am on a short sabbatical before a trip to Chile to set up a new mission there."

"Ah, New Jersey!" Diaz brightened. "My very good friend Bishop McCarrick is there, in Newark. Do you know him?" Diaz stared directly into Don's eyes.

Don didn't flinch. This guy obviously felt it was his duty to look out for Kroslak. Maybe being in the Mexican cartel had taught him not to trust anyone, even a priest, maybe especially a priest. Whatever his reason for prying, Don stood his ground.

"I have heard of the Bishop, though my time there has been short. When I return I will be certain to send your regards should we meet." Don wondered how the hell a Mexican cartel member considered himself good friends with an American Bishop.

Don abruptly turned, looked at Kroslak and said, "A toast to Christmas."

"And to a happy and prosperous new year," Kroslak added gulping the whole glass of wine.

They all raised their glasses, and the conversations resumed, Don being sure to lighten the mood and get the girls to fawn all over the Mexicans again.

A few minutes later, Don knew it was now or never. He pulled in closer to Kroslak and said, "Mr. Kroslak, thank you for the wine and for distributing our flyers, but I can't stay. Could I speak to you in private? There is a message from Father Cabanas about your annual donation to the church."

Bernard laughed out loud, "Sure, I almost forgot. So, that is the reason you came out here tonight!"

Don returned the light laughter. "It's one of the reasons. I hate to be a party pooper, but I have to return to the parish house. Father Cabanas is waiting for me. All of my sins will be forgiven should I return to him with your donation and blessing."

Kroslak laughed, "All right, follow me into my study and I'll write you a check. We don't want to keep the good priest waiting, do we?"

Don followed Kroslak through the main room to a smaller, yet still large room in the front corner. This was Kroslak's study. A large mahogany desk stood in the center of the room. Good, Don thought, plenty of room to maneuver. Several couches and a television formed a separate seating area off to the left, and another bar took up the right corner. Four computer screens sat on top of the desk, and in a back corner was an array of monitors, likely the security system. These were dark though. Don didn't see any cameras. He was ready.

At last they were alone. Kroslak sat down at his desk, took out a checkbook, and began to write. Don pretended to be interested in the souvenirs and artwork lining the walls. He needed to make this happen fast, in case Diaz and his bodyguard really were suspicious and came looking for Kroslak, plus the charges would start going off any minute.

"You have lots of beautiful art." Don commented, keeping up the small talk as he circled behind and then towards the side of Kroslak.

He reached into his coat and took out the knife. Before Kroslak could sign his name on the check, Don rushed forward, subdued him, and with complete accuracy thrust the knife downward through his neck. Blood spurted everywhere and Kroslak sunk to the floor. Don knew time was almost up. He had to act fast to get out of the house and not raise any suspicions. He stuffed Kroslak under the desk so if someone looked in, the room would appear to be empty.

But, before he could get out of the study, the first explosion went off.

It rocked the house.

Chapter 18
THE ESCAPE

DON STAYED CALM and casually walked out of Kroslak's study and quietly closed the door behind him. No one was around. He made his way to the front entrance and opened the floor to ceiling mahogany door with caution in case the guard was there. Behind him he could hear the guests yelling. There was no doubt they were headed towards him and the front door to see what was going on.

Once outside the house, Don could see a huge blaze coming from what used to be the communications building. All the guards in the area were running towards the blaze. He knew he wouldn't be noticed, so he ran across the parking lot to the van and opened the door just as another massive explosion jolted him. That must have been the jet, and all its highly explosive fuel thought Don. A huge fireball from the communications building sent debris falling on the van. He jumped in the van, but Bob wasn't there yet. A slight panic ran through him, and he said a quick prayer, while he was still a priest, that nothing had gone wrong with Bob. The helicopter was supposed to be blown up after the communications building and the jet. He'd give Bob until then before starting to move. He didn't want to be anywhere near the main house when it came time for that to blow.

He started the van, ready to go and watched the scene of chaos. Everyone was running out of the main house now, except for Kroslak of course. He was inspecting the dust underneath his desk. Guards were shouting, guns drawn as they ran towards the explosions. Don saw a couple run the other way. Anxious moments passed. Don knew he couldn't wait much longer. If Bob didn't show he would have to make a plan to come back for reconnaissance later. He couldn't just leave the country without knowing what happened to Bob. Hopefully Bob had his cell and they could meet up outside the ranch if he was stuck or pinned down somewhere. Just as he was about to pull away, the back doors to the van swung open, and Bob jumped in giving a rebel yell saying, "Get the hell out of here!"

As Don hit the gas, more of the guests in the main house were coming outside to see what was taking place. Some were jumping into their cars and heading down the driveway. Others were just standing around, drinks still in their hands. Smoke and ash filled the air and Bob said they had less than one minute to get the hell away before the next explosion. Just then, Hatcher, the bodyguard came running out the front door, gun drawn and pointed right at Don. He must have gone looking for Kroslak and found him. Hatcher was shouting for guards to help him, but they were all too panicked, running towards the explosion. Don stepped on it and they sped down the driveway, heading out towards the main gate. Before he got there he heard the other explosion at the helicopter pad. He looked back without stopping. The house would be next.

Don caught his breath, "Damn, you really know how to spoil a party." They both laughed.

"Did you get Kroslak?"

"Yea, he's dead. It went like clockwork."

"Who was that guy coming at you?" asked Bob.

"That was a cartel thug. Bodyguard of a guy named Diaz who was at the party. I think he was on to me. What do you think?"

"I'd say so," answered Bob. "That can't be good."

Two cars were speeding down the driveway ahead of them, throwing up dust and gravel, but Don wasn't about to slow down. Someone had already run their car through the metal gate at the guardhouse. Don could see the guards through the dust. They looked confused, with no idea what to do. One was waving his arms, trying to stop the vehicles but no one was interested in hanging around the ranch with explosions every couple of minutes.

"Go, go, go," Bob yelled, as Don sped up and right past the two guards who tried to flag them down. Suddenly they heard a volley of gunfire in their direction. A few bullets hit the back of the van. They both got low in their seats and Don pushed the old white van to its limits.

"See ya suckers," Don yelled as he sped through the gate.

As they climbed out of the valley, Bob kept looking back at the flaming complex.

"All hell is about to break loose down there. I found three huge propane tanks beside the main house, set the C-4 charge on them, and opened the valves. When that mother blows it's going to be like an atomic bomb hit them. If there's anyone in or around the house, they're history."

Don tried not to think about the partygoers. Plenty had already left though. Kroslak's body would likely be charred to a crisp by the explosion and fire. Hopefully Diaz would get it too.

It took less than a minute to reach the main road, and when they came around a corner they had one last glimpse of the ranch. You couldn't miss the flames lighting up the surrounding jungle.

"Stop for a minute Don, I want to see what happens with the house. It should go any second."

"Damn, we don't need to admire your work Bob. We need to get out of here. Everyone in Venezuela might be looking for us now."

Don braked and swerved to the side of the road. The main house was about the only thing not on fire. It stood surrounded by burning trees and they could just make out the shape of the jet, fully engulfed.

"Just wait a couple of seconds..." He hadn't finished his sentence when a huge explosion and fireball destroyed the main house. They were almost a mile away and felt the jolt.

"Yes, yes, yes," Bob pumped his fist and let out a big laugh. "I love blowing things up."

Don just smiled at Bob behaving like a teenager.

"Well, that's it. Those cocksuckers deserve what they got. I don't think Kroslak's operation will be doing much in the way of money laundering for the cartels, or arms sales, or dealing in cocaine or anything else anymore. He's in hell now with the rest of his buddies. And by the way, we may have taken out another bad ass too."

"Who's that?"

Don maneuvered out onto the road again.

"That guy, Augustine Diaz. He's a high-ranking member of the Las Zetas Cartel in Mexico. He and his protection, the guy aiming his gun at me at the house, were guests of Kroslak's. They were at the party in deep discussion with Kroslak when I came in. They were here on some big business thing. No doubt about that. I overheard them talking about transferring money from Mexico to Venezuela when I got there. Maybe we foiled a big deal in the making too."

Don pushed the pedal to the floor and sped out of the area.

"OK. Get Manny on the phone now. I'm sure we're heading towards Caracas, but I don't know the location of this damn air strip we're supposed to be flying out of."

Kiser showed him the hand drawn map, as if Don could read it in the dark.

"Santa Rosa is about ten miles from here. Manny said it's five miles north of Santa Rosa. We'll come to an intersection with a small grocery store on the left. He said he tied a white rag to the sign as a signal. There we take a right and go a mile or so down a dirt road. It's a dirt strip that was once used by the local dealers to smuggle drugs in and out of the country, before big timers like Kroslak took over. I guess the bad guys have had to move on so it's pretty much abandoned now. Manny's gonna light up the runway with flares so the plane can land and take off. He should be there waiting for us."

"Oh shit, not another one of those damn propeller, small plane, hair-raising flights. I've been on those too many times."

Bob got Manny on the phone.

"We're coming," was all he said.

They passed a small rusted and faded sign that said, "Santa Rosa 15 KM." At least they were on the right road. Bob had already scoped out the escape route, so he just verified with Manny the directions to the airstrip and that everything was ready for their arrival, and he quickly hung up the phone.

"OK, the plane is there waiting on us now. We're flying straight into Corpus Christi, Texas tonight. No hanging around on this one. With Kroslak's connections here, every cop in Venezuela will be looking for someone to pin this on. It won't take them long to want to talk to good ol' Father James I'm sure."

"Thanks pal, I really needed to hear that shit."

"It'll be OK. Manny's got one of our local contacts waiting. He'll take the van and burn it and destroy the gear so we won't have to worry about the authorities tracing anything back to us."

Don added, "That's good, but remember I'm the one who went in undercover. Father Cabanas at the church could describe me to the police or to some thug. There's plenty of people who've got my number now. Maybe even Augustine Diaz."

For some reason, Don was uneasy about this one and he couldn't hide it.

"So what. You'll be a long way from Santa Rosa, Venezuela," he added, jokingly.

"But hell, you might even have to grow a beard and wear sunglasses for a few months."

They both laughed, glad to have this ordeal behind them. The plane was waiting when they arrived. All three of the elite team shook hands, got into the plane and flew off into the night.

As usual, not much was said on the way back to the states. Manny had managed to stock the small plane with wine and beer. He knew them well. It was dark, there was nothing to look at down below. Don was in deep thought about his future. This was definitely his last mission for the government. This one had been the hardest one yet and Don wasn't interested in working such dangerous and stressful jobs anymore. He wasn't too happy about his level of exposure on this one either. Usually he had little to no contact with anyone but the team when he was in a foreign country. This job had required pretty close contact with several people, starting in Cuba and especially Father Cabanas. Even the guards at Kroslak's compound had seen him enough times to be able to recognize him easily. Any one of the people he had been in contact with, in both countries, could be paid enough to give information, or just have it beaten out of them. Maybe this job had finally cured his need for adrenaline. Maybe he just didn't like being in danger anymore.

If he did choose to leave this line of work after this mission, his life was simplified. He could reflect back on a long and successful career, and he could move on with his life. He thought of his family and of how he would reconnect with them without all the weight on his shoulders. He couldn't help but feel a little panic when he thought about what would have happened if he hadn't made it back from this one. It seemed a real possibility a couple of times. He had never thought of it that way before. He had never really considered the hell his family would have had to endure, if one of these missions had gone wrong. What would his family have to go through if they found out, after he was dead, about the work he was really doing? They'd probably be pretty pissed at him.

So, that was it. He had decided. All of this was just too much to put on them. The double life he had led for so many years was behind him. This is how it had to be from now on. He had some worries about whether he could handle really being in retirement in a month or a year from now. What was he going to do with himself? He'd always been so driven and focused on accomplishment. Could he focus on his family and his personal life the way he focused on a mission or his police work before that? Would he give in to the feeling and get the urge to serve again, should he ever get another call from the government? It would happen. He would be tested. Peter would call again, especially since this one had gone so well. He was sure. At least at this moment he could unequivocally say there was no way. He was done. He would never be involved with the cartels, violence, or danger again.

Still, the old saying came to mind.

Never say never.

Chapter 19
REFLECTIONS

DON GOT BACK to Phoenix in time for Christmas and New Year's. The adjustment to ordinary life was harder this time; he had been gone for much longer than usual and this job was more stressful than any other had been. Processing all the events was slightly easier with the holidays happening. There was plenty of activity, and Diana was home from work for the week, so he did not often find himself alone, having to wrestle with his own thoughts. He worked a little bit at the golf course, but it was still pretty relaxed, even with the winter visitors starting to arrive in big numbers. The busy season was just around the corner, but for now his coworkers were glad to have him back and there was plenty of opportunity for Don to entertain them with his jokes and strange stories. As usual he always had them laughing and that was just what he needed in order to keep the events of the last couple of weeks out of his mind.

As expected the receipt for a deposit into his account by the Department of Agriculture came in the mail. He smiled to himself when he saw the amount he'd been paid for his "farming" services"; teaching new ways of irrigation and planting while in Venezuela. He guessed his priestly days were over, and he just had to shake his head at the craziness of it all. It didn't matter to whoever was depositing the money into his bank account what he had done, how he had done it, or even if he had done it at all. Of course the government would have used their own technology and surveillance to confirm the hit had been made, but no one would talk to Don about the details of how it had gone down. To the government, it didn't matter how these things were taken care of. It only mattered that another drug kingpin was dead and his operation was destroyed enough that it could no longer provide illegal guns and ammunition to dangerous groups and governments. Drugs were part of the currency in their world too. So, taking out one big player would help at least a little bit in the war on drugs. Even if they hadn't taken out the operation completely, it would still take time to rebuild any part of Kroslak's operation, especially with him dead. The government didn't hold Don and the team to specific tasks, the missions were too complicated and risky for that, but all parties involved knew what the ultimate goal was—to eliminate the flow of drugs and weapons—and they were all professionals. If the plan didn't go down perfectly, it was OK, as long as some progress was made in the overall objective. The Department of Agriculture deposit reflected all of the uncertainty, the risk and the personal sacrifice, as well as Don's value as a professional. The cover of providing consulting for farm practices was the perfect set up. He was pretty sure no one at the Department of Agriculture would be checking up on his farming activities in the countries he was sent to.

Winter was the best time in Arizona. The days were sunny and warm compared to those cold, snowy, icy and dark December days in Chicago. No more lake effect snow. No more bitter wind chill that made you cringe when you stepped outside. No more shoveling.

His days were filled with odd jobs around the house, leisurely walks in the neighborhood, and spending quality time with Diana. And, he always had time to spend with his beloved cat, Tommy.

Most people wouldn't think Don was a cat person. After all, he was a cop, a tough guy who told it like it was when it needed to be told. To those on the outside, a big loyal German Shepherd was more the type of pet that matched Don's personality. But, Tommy had won him over from the start. He arrived with attitude. Don liked the way Tommy wasn't focused on pleasing him, or anyone else for that matter. But, Tommy followed Don everywhere. Tommy was tough too and he patrolled the yard as well as any dog. Tommy strutted. And when he was ready for a little quiet time, he'd be right by Don's side—not too cuddly or needy, he would sit next to Don and let him stroke his thick grey coat until he was sufficiently relaxed, and then off he'd go to sleep in the bathtub. At least in summer, that was Tommy's cool spot. In winter he might be inclined to sleep on the end of the bed, but Tommy ran hot and didn't take to too much human warmth.

He had personality too. When someone came to the door, Tommy would come running just like a dog to see who it was. More often than not he'd stand up on his hind legs and put his front paws on the stranger's legs, stretching out long and tall to say hello. More than one cable guy or UPS deliveryman was completely taken with Tommy. He was unique, that was for sure. Tommy was the best companion. Tommy knew it all. And, Tommy could sure keep a secret.

So, Don found himself at his own personal crossroads of sorts. His gut was telling him it was time to quit this line of work. The stress of one more complicated mission like the last one would likely do him in. Besides, while the money was always good, he didn't desperately need it. So, he had to ask himself the hard question. Why was he doing this? He was retired. He had had a long and rewarding career on the police force. He lived in a nice home with good neighbors and friends in a part of the country that had the best weather. He could golf all winter. He could be on the beach in California in a few hours. His life was very good without the government work.

On the Venezuela mission he felt several times he wasn't going to make it out alive. He had felt trapped in the middle of nowhere, surrounded by some extremely dangerous and ruthless criminals who would have taken him out without a second thought, had they discovered his true identity or what he was up to. This wasn't like police work where they all stuck together, supported one another, and had each other's backs when the going got tough. There was no brotherhood. Sure, he and Bob were tight, but not in the same way as guys on the force. Hell, they never even talked about the stuff they did together. Bob went back to his town and Don went to his. Of course, it had to be this way, Don understood, but it didn't make it all any easier. He had felt frustrated by the lack of support on these missions. He didn't mind taking the lead, he preferred it actually, but this one-man show business was pretty risky when you were in a foreign country trying to kill one of its citizens. On one hand, he knew his government appreciated his service, but on the other hand he was invisible to them. It was almost a rejection of sorts, a necessary rejection in order to keep the cover and not create a world news headline, but still the lack of acknowledgement, beyond the pay, for his hard work towards a good cause was at times frustrating.

He was proud of course that he had done the Venezuela job, and he had done it so well. He was nearly certain all the mission objectives had been accomplished. But, he now thought the toll had been too much. The whole picture of his life was suddenly in clear view after Venezuela. Maybe it was because of the timing. Coming home from this tough mission at Christmastime really showed him how good he had it and made him doubt whether the work and the money, and even the adrenaline, were worth it. It had hit him that he could lose it all, or more likely, deeply hurt the lives of Diana and his sons and grandkids if he continued. When he thought of how one failed mission would wreak havoc on so many unsuspecting and innocent people he loved, his path became clear.

One day, as he was out in the yard with Tommy, planting a new lemon tree, it hit him. He leaned on the shovel, bowed his head and accepted the feelings he was having.

"Well Tommy. That's it." Tommy was a good listener.

"Decision made."

He felt relieved to push the doubt and questioning aside. He knew deep down it was time to choose and the choice had been made. He would be done with the government work.

The next time Peter called, he'd tell him that he was retired. Really retired this time. Peter probably suspected as much already anyway. Peter was the one who had offered to Don that Venezuela could be his last mission, no questions asked. Don wasn't sure what life would be like now, but he knew peace and quiet, less stress, was what he was looking for.

His sons and their families couldn't make it for Christmas, but he made a point of talking to all three of them and of getting caught up on their lives. He was happy to hear all the news about his five grandchildren and three great grandchildren. Donny, Michael, and Gary were all doing well with their own lives and families. He was proud of this but knew not to take too much credit for their success. After all, for most of his life he had been somewhat disconnected emotionally from those closest to him. Linda had been the one to figure out what was going on with each of the boys. She was there for them. He did what she told him to do, but something in him from the Vietnam days kept him from really giving himself.

Now finally, he felt he had turned another corner in the long race of his life. There were times when he didn't think he'd ever get to a place where he felt peaceful and at ease. He had always been on the go, ambitious and focused on getting ahead. At some points, he was sure there was something wrong with him, something that kept him from connecting, probably related to all of the horrible events he had witnessed and been a part of. Now, Don felt he could be honest and show his love to his family. He felt some sort of burden had been lifted. For some reason, whatever he had needed from the danger and secrecy and excitement of a mission was now satisfied. He was surprised, as anyone who knew him would be, about the excitement and the contentment, and the feeling of peace, he seemed to be able to tap into now.

In the past he had been somewhat reclusive and had rarely shown any emotion towards his family. He could blame Vietnam or any number of life events for becoming this way, but the reasons didn't matter anymore. It may have taken thirty years or more for him to come to this point, but he was here now. It was the holidays and he didn't want to miss any more opportunities to enjoy the life he had created. So, he spent lots of time with Diana, just enjoying their life. He connected with his sons, and he even called their mother, Linda. Linda had remarried a fine man, and she and Don had settled into a friendly relationship at this point in their lives. He would always be there if Linda needed help, and Don and Diana always visited with Linda's parents when they went back up to Chicago. Don knew he was fortunate they had all been able to put the past behind, and now they were looking to the future.

Just after Christmas Don and Diana took a short trip together and visited Southern California. They flew to San Diego and spent three or four days driving up the coast to Los Angeles where they spent some time touring before they returned home to Phoenix. Don felt the weight off his shoulders. He felt like a new man. Now he just had to put everything behind him, only think of positive things and the times he would like to spend with his family. The future looked very bright indeed.

Chapter 20

SUSPICIOUS ACTIVITY

BACK IN THE desert, the short winter—at least that's what they called it in Arizona with its sixty-degree temperatures and days filled with sunshine—faded into spring. There was no winter, as Don knew it, in Arizona. The intermittent rains of January and February brought the usually dry and barren desert to life. Most people didn't realize how beautiful the desert could be. It always amazed Don how the wildflowers, trees and grasses would suddenly appear once there was little moisture. It was as if all this life was lying dormant, just under the hardscrabble brown dirt and rocks, waiting to sprout into life. Even the cactuses had beautiful vibrant colors. Some mornings he would take a walk and drink in the sounds of the birds enjoying their wintertime respite from the summer heat. The scent of the orange blossoms was something he would always remember, and the Acacia tree with its little round and yellow fuzz balls filled the air with its light perfumed fragrance. But, spring in the desert is short-lived. The relentless sun all-too-soon sends these signs of growth and renewal back underground to avoid the harshness of summer. Don understood this.

One warm afternoon in June Don was trying to stay out of the heat during the hottest part of the day and was watching the U.S. Open golf championship on television. The phone rang. He answered it, but there was silence on the other end of the line, and then the caller hung up. It was annoying since the call came in on the house phone and he'd had to get up to answer it. No one ever called that phone anymore, so he shouldn't have even bothered. The non-call made him renew his goal of getting rid of the house phone; it was only for the telemarketers to annoy him with dinnertime or late-night calls now anyway.

Diana came home from work a little bit early and they made his favorite dinner: meat and potatoes. He'd heard it all about eating healthy, less red meat, more vegetables, and all of that. But, he couldn't help it. He felt like the old dog and he didn't want to learn any new tricks. He liked his old tricks. Thankfully, Diana was not one to push too hard on making him eat differently. She knew how to keep him happy. Besides he was healthy, and unless a doctor gave him some bad news, he'd continue to live the way he always did.

Don and Diana watched the season finale of CSI and a little bit of the late, local Phoenix news. Nothing but murders, robberies, and people behaving badly. Well, except for the token "feel good" story to close out the predictable "newscast." But to Don, it was all life. There were plenty of people who had it hard, and as he knew from his days on the force, anything could happen at any time. It was better people knew about real life through the news, than live in a happy-go-lucky world, one where bad things happened only to other people.

As Diana and Don were getting ready for bed the house phone rang again. Don was brushing his teeth, so Diana answered. It was late, even for a telemarketing call, and when Don heard the ring he rushed through brushing, intending to give whoever or whatever company was on the other end of the line a piece of his mind. Jesus! It was nearly 11:00 p.m. What gave them the right to call at this hour?

But, when he came out of the bathroom Diana had already hung up the phone.

"Did you give them hell for calling at this hour?" he fumed.

"There was no one to give hell to, there was just silence."

Don stopped, but then moved towards the bed. "Yeah, that happened earlier today too," he said. "The computers must be messed up. We need to get rid of that phone number. No one but sales people ever call it anyway."

This is what Don said to Diana, but inside this call had created turmoil. He had told Peter he was through just the month before. While it was hard, Don had no regrets. He knew he was finally relaxing into his life and not always sitting around on edge waiting for another phone call. Peter understood and even told him there would be a final bonus payment heading Don's way to thank him for his service. Don guessed it was a retirement gift of sorts. But, though he had given up his dangerous way of life, his guard would never go down. He was too well trained, and he knew too much about how the dark side of this life worked to ever stop paying attention to his surroundings. It was just a smart way to live. He had spent his life on guard, protecting, looking for clues and patterns in the things that seemed like coincidences, and that way of thinking would never leave him no matter how retired he became. He slept that night, but only after much tossing and turning and running through all sorts of scenarios in his mind. His first thought upon waking was he needed to pay close attention to everything that was going on, and he would need to keep up on what Diana was doing and with whom. Something inside was not sitting right. He had an uneasy feeling in his gut and he had lived long enough, and been through enough, to know he should listen to it.

At the golf course the next day he was ready when the first twosome, two guys named Carlos Rica and Fernandez Lopez, arrived to hit the course. They were getting an early tee time to beat the heat. He assigned them a golf cart and sent them on their way with a few good-natured comments to get them started. That's what Don did, and why the golf course loved him. He made the people happy. He kept the workers up and in a good mood and that led to happier customers. For Don, this was a cushy job, no pressure like his other positions. So, he found it easy to be light hearted and to enjoy the days at the course. Of course, Don was always that way anyway, even while on the force, but here he wasn't pretending. With this job, his good nature came a lot more easy and natural. He wasn't making much but it kept him busy and entertained, and out of trouble.

After their eighteen holes, the two men returned and chitchatted with Don about the weather and how nice the course had played. Don learned they were from Los Angeles, in town for a medical convention at one of the Hilton resorts in Phoenix.

"Do you live around here?" one of them asked.

Don never had his guard down and he didn't offer any specifics.

"Yeah, I live in the Valley. Great place to spend the winter, but it's getting a little too warm now. We should top one hundred again today."

"Do you work here fulltime?" They continued to make conversation. They asked if he was married, had kids, pets. All the while, Don was telling little white lies and trying to steer the conversation towards an end. He was not one to open up. Maybe he had been too well trained. He had learned to not trust people, especially strangers, and he just didn't like their curiosity about him. These kinds of people always made him feel uncomfortable, especially with the uneasiness he had already been feeling in his gut about the phone calls the night before. If they were women it would have been different. But, Don had an inherent distrust of guys like this who were a little to nosey, especially those he didn't know. Maybe it was all of his training and experience, maybe it was just who he was, but he was not comfortable with their attempts at small talk.

But, they must have felt pretty comfortable with Don, or they were trying to make him feel that way, because he didn't expect the next question.

"Would you know a place we could pick up some chicks tonight?" one of them asked.

Aha! Maybe this is what they were trying to get around to with all their small talk. Well, Don was more than happy to switch the topic off him and on to strippers.

"That depends on what you're looking for." Everything

about him warmed up towards the new direction of the conversation. He felt his jovial, relaxed side kick in.

"Some real good looking girls who could…say…enjoy the night with us."

Of course Don knew all the hotspots around the valley, but he thought of one club in particular where the girls were professional escorts. These guys were obviously well off, and this place was a little more upscale than some of the run-of-the-mill strip joints lining Scottsdale Road. He figured they had some money to burn, and he knew where they were sure to be shown a real good time.

Don smiled, "Try Christie's Cabaret over on Baseline Road. It's what you're looking for. I highly recommend it," he said with a wink.

"Hey thanks a lot, we really appreciate it."

They shook Don's hand then swung their clubs across their backs and walked back to the clubhouse. Well that was a little weird, but it had ended well. More happy customers. Still, something was unsettled in Don.

The rest of the afternoon passed uneventfully. That evening, just as he had settled into his easy chair, the house phone rang again. Diana was on her way home from work so he answered, plus he was curious to find out what would happen if he answered. As before, there was silence on the other end and then the all too familiar click, as the caller hung up. The anger rose in him and he slammed the phone down onto the receiver.

Just then, he heard Diana's car in the driveway. He took a couple of deep breaths as she came into the kitchen carrying a bag of groceries. She plopped them on the counter.

"Hi honey, how was your day?" she asked coming over to him and giving him a kiss on the cheek.

"Not too busy…just a few golfers. It's slowing down with the hotter weather." Don slid into his Don-the-husband mode.

"I stopped at the store and found us a couple of beautiful filets and a bottle of red." She knew what he liked. He reached for the bottle to open the wine right away. It would help him think.

"Good, I'm famished. Do you want me to light up the grill?"

"In a few minutes," she said, as she was unpacking. "I'm going to go get cleaned up first. Oh, and I met the nicest man at the vegetable section in the grocery store just now."

Don had moved into the living room and was trying to concentrate on the evening news while calming down about the phone call.

"Yeah, and who was that?"

"Well, I didn't get his name or anything. I was picking out asparagus and he was too. He was Latino and he gave me a great recipe for them, with a cheese sauce topping. Not spicy. I told him how you didn't like spicy. We had a nice chat in line at the checkout and he even carried my groceries to the car for me. You just don't see men like that these days."

"Did he say anything else?"

"No, not really. He asked a lot about me, which I thought was strange, but maybe we are all just too paranoid these days. Whenever a stranger is nice to us, we automatically get suspicious. I don't want to be that way. He was a very nice man."

Don had to chuckle. He wasn't a jealous man.

"You fell for an old trick, honey. He probably wanted to get you into the sack. Some men hang out at the grocery store to pick up women you know."

The chuckle was not real, and the unsettled feeling only deepened.

Chapter 21
PANIC

DON DIDN'T SLEEP well. A gut feeling was gnawing at him. Something was wrong. He could feel it. All of his extensive training and experience had taught him to pay attention, and the seemingly benign and unconnected events of the past few days were suddenly making him nervous. He couldn't quite put his finger on it yet, but he had learned enough in his life to know when to listen to that uneasy feeling inside. He'd made plenty of mistakes in the past when he ignored it and just ploughed on ahead, status quo. Call it experience. Call it age, but this time he couldn't, and knew he shouldn't, ignore what was going on.

The next day he needed to get out of the house to clear his thoughts. As he was driving to the pharmacy, about three miles away, he noticed a black Buick in his rear view mirror, and he was suddenly suspicious it was following him. There were two men in the car, but he couldn't make out their faces. He took a couple of turns and came at the pharmacy from a different direction, and sure enough, the Buick followed him. When he returned to the main road the Buick kept its position, well back, but behind him nonetheless. Once at the strip mall where the pharmacy was located, he turned into the parking lot. The Buick passed by before he could get out of his car, but he caught a glimpse of the passenger, and he was certain he was a Latino guy.

Immediately a red flag popped into his mind. He had the definite feeling someone or something was closing in on him. Someone was definitely tailing him. Hell, he had tailed suspects hundreds of times. He knew how it went. This wasn't a coincidence. Who in the hell was following him? He knew, because of his career as a police officer and his time with the elite squad, that there were many reasons for him to be concerned. He'd put enough people away to be worried something was coming back on him. His police detective side practically screamed at him that something suspicious was going on, but he couldn't quite put his finger on it yet.

He reviewed the last two days events in his mind again. He remembered the Latino golfers at the golf course who seemed a bit overly friendly and curious about Don's personal life. And, all the hang-ups on his home phone were still in the back of his mind. He had the distinct feeling someone was casing him, trying to find out his patterns and his routines. Don decided he needed to do a little of his own investigating to try to put his mind at ease. Before going into the pharmacy, he picked up his cell phone and found the number for the Hilton Hotel.

"Yes, I'm trying to find a friend of mine," he told the receptionist. "Is there a medical convention booked there this week?"

"Let me check," she clicked him onto hold and smooth jazz filled his ear. He hated jazz. It didn't help his anxiety one bit.

"No sir. There are no medical conferences at this time."

"Have you had a medical convention in the last week?"

"No sir. I don't believe we have. The whole hotel was taken up last week by a real estate convention."

"OK. Thanks."

He hung up. That call had not put his mind at ease. In fact, it made the feelings of anxiety worse. But, at least he now had his own information. He knew now the two golfers had lied. When he put it all together in his mind, suddenly panic flew all over him. He was certain now danger was afoot. Someone was after him, and there was no more time to question and doubt his gut. His first thought was to call Diana at work.

"Listen Diana, the Latino guy you met at the grocery store. Did he see you leave in your car?"

"I guess so. We went out of the store together. He carried my groceries. Why?"

"Oh nothing. I'm just the jealous type I guess. It's nothing. I'll see you when you get home."

Sitting in his car in the parking lot of Walgreen's, he ran over it all again. The phone calls, the fake doctors at the golf course, the grocery store man, and now the Buick following him around. Someone was watching him and his wife and he didn't like the possibilities. Diana was safe enough for now, working at the police station. Damn, was someone from his past out to get him? He flew out of the parking lot and headed back to his house without even going into the pharmacy. He now felt he had to arm himself fast and make a call to the local police, who he hoped would listen to his suspicions and not think he was just a crazy man. Most of all he had to make a plan. He needed more information. Panic was not going to get him anywhere.

When he got home he went straight to the bedroom closet, grabbed his Beretta and loaded the clip. He checked all the windows and doors in the house. Automatically, he was in a defensive mode, checking out every angle in case he was attacked at his home. He rechecked the settings and the code to the burglary alarm. He cursed himself for getting soft. He used to be pretty good about keeping his guard up, even at home. But now, in semi-retirement, he hadn't thought about his own, or his family's protection in quite a while. He had no Plan B for getting out and keeping both he and Diana safe. Sure, he could secure the house pretty fast, but their lifestyle was wide open. Their patterns, their routines, they had settled in pretty comfortably in Arizona, and any thoughts of someone trying to harm them had faded away. He figured no one knew him here. Looking for ways to relieve the panic, he called the local police department and spoke with a Detective Hennessey.

"Detective, this is Don Ballantine. I'm a retired investigator from Chicago. I think I have a situation on my hands. It may sound crazy, but I'm pretty sure someone is out to get me."

"What do you mean, kill you?"

"Yes." Don relayed all he knew so far; the fake doctors, the hang-ups, the grocery store incident and the black Buick that was obviously tailing him. He tried to make it sound as professional as he knew how, hoping Hennessey would hear that Don was not just reading into things, that he was on to something serious.

Hennessey's response was not wholly unexpected.

"Don, of course we'll help you in any way we can, but until a crime is committed there's not much to go on here."

"I don't want to wait for a crime to be committed, Detective. I want some kind of protection. I especially want my wife protected."

"The best we can do right away is put a squad car on your street. In the meantime, if anything suspicious occurs let me know immediately and we'll respond. Could this be one of the guys you sent to prison, out for revenge?"

"I'm not sure, it's possible. I'll have to think of all the ones who might be suspect."

"You do that. If you can give us some names we can have them checked out, maybe find their whereabouts. And in the meantime, we'll have a squad car patrolling your street 24/7, when we can. Just try to relax and dig up something else to go on. But, whatever you do, don't take this on yourself. We're here to help if we can get a lead."

"Thanks, Detective." Don hung up frustrated, but maybe more with the truth than with Detective Hennessey.

Don didn't need to think too hard about the root of this problem or what he feared was the truth. Of course, he couldn't tell the detective about his work for the government. He was sworn to secrecy about any of those missions, but that was the source foremost on his mind. In the past couple of years, he had killed some pretty serious criminals with very long reaches. Could one of the cartels actually have figured out who he was and come to seek revenge? Knowing what he knew about the cartels, this thought put a deep sense of dread over Don. He knew if this was true they would stop at nothing to get him and his family. But how could they possibly have tagged him? The only job he could think of was Caracas. It was the only job that put him in direct contact with so many cartel members and local people. Between Cuba, Caracas, and the little village of Santa Rosa, he had met quite a few people while he was posing as Father James. It seemed possible now that the undercover priest tactic may not have been enough to protect him.

He wanted to contact someone in the government, maybe one of his FBI connections, to let them know of his concerns, but he didn't expect any assistance from them. He didn't even know what he would say to them since everything was a secret.

He thought about the team. Were they in danger too? He had a phone number for Bob Kiser. Bob had given it to him privately, since they had known each other for so long. If Bob wasn't out on another mission, maybe he could help. He had no way of contacting Manny Perez. Usually Peter contacted the team individually. As far as Don knew, no one knew how to contact Peter, and Peter was very stealth during and after the training sessions. Don realized he really knew nothing about Peter at all, and he knew deep down anyway Peter could be of no help to him. He'd been told that enough times.

Don tried to think of anyone he could to turn to. Even his friends in the FBI didn't know of his missions. The Secret Service was involved, but he had no contacts there.

He remembered the two suits at the Venezuela briefing, but those guys hadn't even given a first name. Damn, it seemed to come down to what he was told when he signed up; you are on your own, with no government backing of any kind. But, despite that reality, Don couldn't help but become even more frustrated. He was after all in the United States, in his own city, at his home. Surely, someone would listen to him as an American citizen possibly being threatened. But, if he told the truth to someone, someone official, what would happen? What can of worms would be opened if he admitted to someone what he had done in the name of service to his country? His thoughts spiraled as he thought about Diana and his family. This was a hell of a way for them to find out what he had been up to since moving to Arizona and retiring. What had he gotten them into? Maybe he wasn't yet prepared to spill out the truth either. There had to be another way to handle this.

It hadn't happened yet, but he had this gut feeling someone was after him, and because his thoughts kept coming back to the missions, he had a pretty good idea of who it might be.

He called Diana at work. He tried not to sound worried, but he was.

"Hi honey. Listen. Don't ask me any questions right now, but I want you to come straight home after work tonight. No stops. Just come straight home, okay?"

"OK, but is something wrong?"

"Everything's fine. I'll tell you all about it when you get home, but I need you to come straight home."

He wanted to tell her to take a different route, but he

thought this might put her over the edge. Besides, that would probably be an overreaction anyway.

"Of course. OK. You have me worried now though."

"Don't worry. I'm fine. You're fine. I've got it all under control. I just need to talk to you about a few things when you get home. We'll have a nice dinner too. I'll take something out now." He tried to change the subject so she wouldn't start asking questions.

Though he had now made Diana worry too, he had a growing feeling they should all be worried. He wasn't sure how to break the news to her. They both might be in serious danger.

Chapter 22
ASSISTANCE

IT WAS A long day. But, Don needed the time to think. He needed to figure out his options and he needed a plan. Diana was safe at work for now. It was as pretty safe bet no one was going to attack the local police station just to get at her. This was the worst part of it all, knowing Diana was in danger too. The thought of that scumbag talking to her at the grocery store made him rage inside. If he ever figured out who that guy was he would beat the crap out of him. It made his head spin to think something could have already happened to Diana, that day. And it was all his fault. The guilt lay heavily on his mind. But, he would get her out of Phoenix as soon as possible. He knew she would not be happy, but he'd convince her it was the right thing to do, without letting on exactly how dire he was beginning to think the situation was.

By late morning he had secured the house from easy entry and secured himself with the Berretta, and he had come up with a plan to get Diana out. She wasn't going to like it, but he knew it was how it had to be. Now the question was how he could get himself on the offensive instead of staying at home feeling like a sitting duck. He was fairly certain they'd try to hit him here, at home. That's what he would do. They probably already knew he didn't have any routines, he didn't go anywhere except to the golf course, and even that was sporadic right now.

By late afternoon Don had had enough of pacing the floor, observing the street outside, and looking for suspicious vehicles. He didn't like to have to do it, but he decided to call Bob Kiser. If anyone could help him get out of this, if anyone could understand the seriousness of the situation, it was Bob. In fact, he knew Bob was the one and only person he could call. He dialed the number he had, but got an answering machine with a nondescript voice. He left a normal message, one without panic, or any identifying information. But, Bob would know who it was.

He had no idea what city he was calling, but it was in the 626 area code. All he could do now was wait for him to return the call. Don felt like he needed backup and he needed it immediately. Who knew when these thugs would strike? Don knew, from being on the other side, if they were following him and checking out his house, they weren't going to wait much longer before making their move. From what little information Don had pieced together up to this moment, they already knew the situation enough to act. They were close, and he'd done the same thing enough to know that swiftness was an ally in these situations.

With a sigh of relief, he spotted Diana's car pulling into the driveway. She came into the house and he met her at the door.

"What is going on Don? I don't understand what you're so upset about."

"It's a long story, so you better have a seat," he said nervously.

She moved into the living room and took a seat on the sofa, watching Don as he looked out the window to see if she had been followed. Finally, he took a seat beside her, took a deep breath, and began to explain.

"First of all, and most importantly, I love you, and my first goal in life is to take care of you and to protect you. I would never let anything bad ever happen to you. But, we have a problem. I suspect some very bad men are out to get me. Some things have happened this week that add up to trouble, and I need to handle it."

"What do you mean? What things?"

"Do you remember the hang up phone calls, the man at the grocery store, and the two Latino men asking questions about me at the golf course? Well, I found out the golfers where fake. They lied to me about why they were in Phoenix. The guy at the grocery store was definitely trying to get information out of you and likely identifying your car. And, this morning when I was out doing errands, two men were tailing me. Something is going on, I know it, and I think it has something to do with some very violent people I've had to deal with in the past, back in Chicago. That's got to be it. I helped send some of them to prison, and I'm sure they still think I ruined their lives and their families' lives. They don't care about the crimes they committed, and it's possible they are seeking revenge. I don't know who might be after me, but there are only one or two I can think of that might have it in for me."

At that moment Don just couldn't go into his government work and the missions he was sent on in Central and South America. It would probably come out later, but for now he had to make shit up to help Diana understand the severity of the immediate problem. He didn't want to shock her too much with the truth about his own double life.

"So what are you saying? How can you be sure someone is here in Phoenix? Can't you contact the police department and get some protection for us? I can talk to someone at work and get some help for us."

"No, no, don't do that. I've already contacted the Mesa Police, and all they can do right now is patrol our street and keep a lookout for suspicious people. Nothing has happened yet. No laws have been broken yet. I'm working with them to ID the guys, and then the police can make a move. We first need to figure out where these guys are from."

Diana was getting anxious now. "What are we supposed to do? Just sit here and wait and hope nothing happens?"

"Not we honey. This is my fault and my problem. I've thought about it long and hard and I don't want any argument about it. You have a cousin in Long Beach. Until this blows over, I think you should take some time off and stay with her while I work this thing out."

"Oh Don." Diana groaned, visibly upset now. "This is nuts. I don't want to leave you. How can I just suddenly take off from work? What will I say? I don't want to leave. There has to be another way to handle this. Who can we call? Is this the only solution?"

"I don't want you here honey. If it gets dangerous, I can take care of myself, but if I have you to protect also, it's only going to make things harder for me."

"But what about you? Who's going to protect you?" she asked.

Don ignored the question.

"Believe me, I wouldn't ask this of you if there was any other way. The people I'm talking about are mean, vicious, and violent criminals who have a grudge against me. It may take a little time, but we'll get these sons-of-bitches if it's the last thing I do."

"Don, you're scaring the hell out of me with that kind of talk. And, who's we? Do you have help?"

Just then the phone rang. "I have to take this in private, honey. You need to go pack a few things. Take enough for a week, just in case." He took the phone out onto the patio. Tommy followed him out.

"What's up Don? This is Bob Kiser."

There was no time for pleasantries.

"Listen buddy, I have a situation out here in Arizona. I need your help and I mean fast. I'm positive someone is out to get me. Looks like a couple of Latino guys. They're watching me and my wife, and they're getting pretty close. At this point I would guess they're just waiting for the right moment to kill me."

"Any idea who these dudes are?"

"I've wracked my brain and no one comes to mind except people involved in our job down in Venezuela. It's the only thing that makes sense. I knew that place was nothing but trouble and I think that old priest, Father Cabanas, may have fingered me as the one who killed his drug dealing buddy Kroslak."

"I hate to say it, but that makes some sense." Bob agreed.

"Of all the missions we've been on, Cabanas is the only one who could provide a good description of me. I can't think of another possibility, or another group that would have such reach. I have a good hunch these guys watching me want to kill me for what we did down there."

"Shit Don, those guys don't play around. OK, my advice to you at the moment is to go into hiding until I get there. Maybe, just maybe, we can put together a plan to get rid of them somehow. Shit, I'm sure there's a hefty price on your head if you're right, and these guys are probably hardcore."

"Tell me about it. I get it. I can't believe this is happening, but I'm not crazy. It is happening and I need some backup."

"No problem. I'll be there tomorrow afternoon. Get rid of your wife and find some place to go until then. Don't pick me up at the airport. Give me your address and I'll find my way to your house. We don't want to tip them off in any way. Just stay low and hang in there."

Diana was in the kitchen tidying up.

"Sorry about the interruption. That was my backup. I need to get you out of here first though."

"Well, I need to arrange it Don. I can't just show up at my cousin's unannounced."

"I've already set it up. I'm sorry. I called her already. I can't have any argument about this. I need you to pack whatever you need and be prepared to leave in an hour," he told her.

"An hour?" This really pissed her off.

"Can't I just go in one last day and wrap things up?"

"I don't think it's a good idea. Just call in sick tomorrow. I called Detective Hennessey at the police department and he's sending a squad car here to escort you out of town. It's still early and you can make the drive out there easily now that it's cooled down. When you get to your cousin's house lay low for a few days. Don't call me on the home phone because they can trace the call. I'll use my cell phone to call you to make sure you made it."

"Don, I don't like this at all. I think I should stay here with you."

"No way. Please. Just do it my way this time. I know what we're dealing with and I don't want you anywhere near it. Tommy's going with you too. He'll keep you company on the ride."

Diana was visibly upset but did as asked. She sensed enough not to push Don on this, and she had enough faith and trust in him to know the best thing she could do right now was to do whatever he needed.

The squad car arrived in an hour as planned. Diana put her bags into her car and followed the squad car out of the neighborhood. Don was relieved to see her get out of harm's way. When he went back inside the empty house, he felt more alone than any time in his life. Time to think was not a good thing. The realization this was really happening to him hit him hard, over and over.

Chapter 23
PROTECTION

DON DIDN'T GO anywhere. He didn't go into hiding as Bob had suggested. He wasn't going to hide from these guys. But, he knew he needed to wait for Bob's help, so he put the car in the garage, didn't turn the lights on when it became dark, and he made it appear that no one was home. Of course, he was up all night, pacing back and forth to the front windows, and keeping watch on the street for the black Buick or any other suspicious vehicle.

The long night gave him plenty of time to review his past cases while at the police department, but no one person or case came to mind that would explain someone coming after him down in Arizona. There was one guy that was an outside shot. He was a pretty tough and scary motherfucker that had been running a good-sized drug operation back in Chicago. He'd already done plenty of time, so he had that ex-con attitude of not giving a shit about anyone or anything. They'd been watching him for months, maybe over a year, but couldn't get the break that would put him away. But, like most of the small timers do, he made a big mistake one night.

He crossed the wrong person: his girlfriend. Relationships were usually the downfall of guys who thought they were tough and in control. That old saying about the fury of a woman scorned was the truth. She was as tough as he was, but one night he beat the crap out of her one too many times and she turned on him. She called the police, and when Don, his partner, and about twenty other officers, showed up, Don knew they had him. It was a pretty good feeling to nail him with all the drugs found in the apartment, and now knowing all the evidence they had about the larger operation would now stick. This guy was going away for a good long time, Don was sure of that. Maybe Don was a little too cocky, but this guy was a real asshole and Don let him know it. First, for beating his woman, and second, for being part of the problem of good kids losing their lives because of the drugs that he supplied. A few extra well-placed kicks let the guy know how Don really felt about him. Of course, this really pissed him off, and later in court the guy sent daggers through his eyes and mouthed death threats at Don. Don let all his emotions out for the court record, and while on the stand, he didn't hold back the contempt he had for this piece of shit. He was sent away for thirty years, but who knows if somehow he got out early. They were letting a lot of these drug guys out now. Even if he wasn't out, he could have sent someone on the outside to take his revenge on Don. Even so, even as bad as that guy was, Don was pretty sure he didn't have the deep desire he'd need, or the wherewithal, to organize a hit on Don down in Arizona.

No, Don knew in his gut these guys had to be from South America or Central America. Whenever the team had operated down there they had always been very conscious of having no witnesses when they took down the bad guys. They barely had any contact with anyone and of course this was on purpose. There were no parties, just quiet dinners in the hotel where they were staying. Except for Manny. Besides the fiasco of the girl he had ended up with, he usually set up the local contacts to take care of the cleanup operations. He knew a lot of locals because he had to. But, Don hardly spoke to anyone on these trips. Of course, they were all cautious because they never wanted anyone to be able to trace them back to the States. But, now it seemed this was exactly what was happening.

Usually, they were in and out of a country so fast that there was no time for fraternizing with the locals. No one ever suspected them of anything. They were just there to teach farming techniques to the locals. Even Manny's local contacts in a country were close-mouthed about assisting the team in eliminating their targets. The contacts knew they were risking everything, and should they ever be discovered by the cartel, they and their family would have been killed too. All of the operations, and everyone involved knew the stakes, and this kept everyone in line, as far as Don knew. But, there was one trip that had been different. He had been in Venezuela for a long time compared to the other missions. And, he had had repeated contact with several people there. This was Don's worst nightmare come true.

Again, he narrowed it down to the Venezuela incident. It absolutely had to be Father Cabanas or perhaps the guy Manny hired, the one who had destroyed the van and the weapons after they left the country. He had seen them at the airport. The pilot had had a good look at Don and the crew too. But, these two didn't have a high stake in anything that had gone on down there. Father Cabanas was a different story though. He had lost a lot and could surely identify Don easily; they had spent quite a bit of time together. With Kroslak dead, Cabanas lost his sole source of funding. Don was pretty sure the good father knew a lot more than he had let on, and it was likely underneath the priest clothes, he was the eye-for-an-eye type.

Don was frustrated with himself. He was frustrated with Peter and the government too. He should have spoken up for himself more, maybe pushed for some better disguise. Even if he'd grown a beard and mustache or dyed his hair, it might have thrown off anyone now looking for him. He had never become so close to the locals either. Compared to other missions, he had been totally exposed in Venezuela. Handing out flyers all across the valley, playing the part of the friendly priest, he was good at it, but now it might just be biting him in the ass. The locals he had met loved him. He couldn't count the number of houses he was invited into for snacks or coca tea. But all thoughts returned to the most likely source, the quiet and meek head of the local church who pretended not to know anything about what was going on. Don had always felt a little uneasy with Father Cabanas. It always felt as if Cabanas suspected something. Whoever it was that had identified Don, it seemed that they had tracked him down in Phoenix, and now he was the target.

Don had done enough research to know the dangerous position he was in. He spent the night doing more research because he felt strongly the more he knew the better he could protect himself. The cartels were more active in the United States each year. According to some reports, the cartels supplied nearly all of the cocaine, heroin, and methamphetamines on the streets of the U.S. With the growing problem of drug addiction, the United States was the best market for the South American cartels and they'd stop at nothing to keep things running smoothly. Throughout his career, Don recalled reading about hits by the cartel in places like Chicago, the big cities, but now he was reading how, increasingly, the cartels were moving into quiet places. Nowadays, a cartel hit in Minnesota or South Carolina, or even Arizona was not unheard of. The news didn't make a big deal of these crimes. Who knows why, but it was happening, and Don was likely now the target of the cartel's violent tactics, used to keep control of their cash cow: drugs.

The cartels were probably moving their activities to the smaller cities and towns because of the crackdown in the larger cities. They knew they could more easily get away with killing those that turned on them in places like Oregon than they could in New York City. Don read one story of a guy in Oregon who was killed at point-blank range by the cartel. He was found in his SUV, right in his own driveway, shot dead. No one saw anything. No one heard anything. At least they weren't saying if they did.

The research didn't help. It only made Don more nervous. The cartels were likely well- embedded in the Phoenix area. This is what Don feared. While Phoenix was close to Mexico, cartel activity was still not high on the radar of the local police. Detective Hennessey was proof of that. Though Don couldn't tell him everything, what he did tell him should have set off some flags and had Hennessey digging deeper. Instead, all Don got was, "call me if something real happens."

Don knew the cartels would use any and all means of finding and eliminating people who turned on them: people that stole, ratted, or tried to branch out on their own. And, if they had figured out Don was the guy who had murdered one of their leaders, then there was no question that they would look to return the favor on this side of the border. They were masters of covering their tracks, of getting in and out, and of getting the job done. The thugs that were following him probably lived in the United States and worked for the cartels. There would likely be no airline ticket trail for these guys. Hell, he thought, even if they were in Mexico, they wouldn't even need a ticket from Arizona. A quick midnight drive across some lonely, unwatched border road would put them back in Mexico with all the protection they could want.

Don also thought these men could have been sent by Augustine Diaz, the top ranking member of the Pacific Cartel and Kroslak's party guest that night—if he had survived the attack. Don wasn't sure if Diaz had lived or died when the explosion destroyed the main house at Kroslak's complex; he hadn't stuck around to find out. Whatever the case, someone had lived long enough to talk and these guys were here stalking Don now. He had to defend himself or most likely be killed. It was going to be a long day until Bob Kiser arrived and they could make a plan. He would just have to hope that without any activity around the house, they'd assumed he was not home. To be safe, he would go out late morning and stay out until afternoon. He'd stay in public places with lots of people around. Maybe he would go hang out at the golf course.

It was hard to keep the guilt and anger at bay and focus on what he needed to do to end this situation, in his favor. All of this was happening because of his actions. The worst-case scenario was coming to fruition. It was a slippery slope down to anger, and depression, and regret, and he was sliding fast. He had to do something to occupy his mind. He tried to focus on how he could get a leg up on the situation. Action was always a good cure for anxiety and depression. He called a friend at the FBI office in Quantico. He asked him to contact immigration and see if any known cartel members had entered the United States from Venezuela recently. The agent said he'd call him back later that day with any information.

This was going to be a waiting game and Don didn't feel time was on his side. These guys had gotten pretty close to him already, and they could attempt the hit any time now. All Don could do was wait for Bob to help him and try to protect himself in the meantime. He looked at his handgun and shook his head. The Beretta was not much of a defense against criminals who have every weapon imaginable at their disposal, including automatic assault rifles. He had flashbacks of the firefights in Vietnam when a whole division of the enemy had them under attack. They were out-manned and out-gunned, but they had survived. Once again, the enemy was on him and the odds were about the same.

Chapter 24

TRACK DOWN

FINALLY, JUST BEFORE sundown a taxi pulled along curbside in front of Don's house. He was relieved to see his reliable partner, Bob Kiser getting out of the car with a small duffle bag across his shoulder. They'd sure been through a lot together starting with the FBI academy. It wasn't your conventional friendship, but it was solid. As Bob came up the walkway, looking around to see if anyone was watching, Don was grateful to have him to turn to in what seemed to be becoming a dire situation. Don opened the door.

"Welcome to Phoenix. It's been a while, but I'm sure as hell glad to see you."

"Anything to help a brother," Bob said in his gruff voice.

They grabbed a couple of sodas; alcohol would do no good right now, and settled at the kitchen table to brainstorm. Don recounted the series of events that had happened in the past few days. He tried to stick just to the facts, but found it tough since his own life seemed to be on the line. When he had all the information, Bob was quiet for a moment. He could see Don was rapidly heading into a state of panic, and rightfully so. The situation was grim and sugar coating it was not going to save their lives.

"Listen my friend, we both know when the cartels and gangs are out to get you they usually succeed. There's no time limit on when it will occur, they are relentless and stop at nothing. But don't forget, we have the advantage here. It does sound like these guys are dogging you for a reason. I think you're right on with what you're thinking. There's a connection. They know where you live, they know your car, they know Diana's car and where she shops. They've been calling and hanging up, or having someone else do it, so they can get a feel for when you're home, how late you're up, when Diana's here, and all that. It sounds like they're just waiting for the right time to try to take you out."

Don's face turned grim, "I think there are two of them and maybe a third; the guy in the grocery store must be working with them. From Diana's description, he was a lot older than the two pricks at the golf course and the ones in the Buick."

"Well, the first thing is we've got to find out more about them. Maybe the older guy is the leader. Maybe he's training the younger two. I think we can give them a pretty good lesson though. They really have no idea who they've decided to pick a fight with," Bob said.

"So, let's review. You suspect the men from the golf course, who were supposedly at a medical convention, are not who they said they were?"

"Yes, they're in their thirties, black hair, lean built, clean cut Latinos."

"And that day you told them to visit some strip club for

women while they were in town?"

Bob was formulating a plan. Don was suddenly thankful for his presence and having someone to talk things over with—someone with a clear mind who could calm him down and put a plan into motion. It was the only way. For the first time in over twenty-four hours he took a deep breath and relaxed just a little a bit. This was helping him to think clearer, and that's what he needed in order to use all his knowledge, training, and experience to get him and Diana, and now Bob, out of this mess.

"That's right, at the time I thought they were just a couple of guys here at a convention, but I found out later that was a lie. There was no medical convention here. So, I believe these are the two guys that have been tailing me in a black Buick."

"And have you contacted the police here?"

"Yes, but it's the usual bull shit. They really can't do anything until a crime is committed. They did send a squad car out here to escort Diana out of town, but that was just a favor to me as an ex-cop. She's staying with a relative till this thing blows over."

"Well, the first thing is your car. We can't use it. It's an easy target for them. Can you arrange to get a rental here ASAP?"

"Good idea. No problem, I'll make the call over to Enterprise and they'll deliver it here."

"I think I'll pay a visit to Christie's and ask a few questions. Maybe these characters took your advice and went there. I'm sure a little green will get me something on them. Hopefully, I can get a lead on their whereabouts; maybe where they're staying or something. I think it's time we started tailing them instead of them tailing you. Are you packing heat?"

Don went into a kitchen drawer and retrieved the weapons and ammo. He handed Bob a Glock, and he kept his trusty Beretta. He'd had plenty of time to get them in good shape and for one of the first times since being in Arizona, he was glad he kept weapons in the house. This was no time to be lining up a gun purchase.

"OK, you stay here so no one sees you. Stay inside and try to calm down. You know the drill. Keep the lights off. Keep away from the windows. Have an escape plan out the back and out the front. These guys probably don't know we're onto them and they could just be waiting, ready to strike at any time. I know you're ready, but I sure hope you don't have to do it alone. I'll be as fast as I can. I should be back in an hour or two. Don't worry we're going to track these guys down."

"Sure, you go out to the club while I stay home and clean the house like the good little wife," Don's sense of humor made a comeback.

"That's right and I don't want any crap about it."

Don and Bob had their first real laugh since Bob had arrived. It felt good. This was how they did things. It was serious, but humor helped them both to think straight and to focus on the task at hand.

The rental car arrived and Bob headed towards the club. Again, Don was left alone and despite trying to stay calm, he was getting more paranoid by the minute. Every little sound he heard around the house and outside, he investigated, ready to use the Beretta at any time. He wished he had gone with Bob, just to get out of the house.

Bob entered the topless club and the typical dark, smoke

filled room. On the stage a girl was gyrating around a pole with a dozen or so men pressed against the stage, gawking at her. He moved to the bar and ordered a red wine from the beautiful blonde topless bartender. Just in case, he surveyed the room for anyone meeting Don's description of the two Latinos and saw no one fitting the bill. Of course, that was a long shot, but sometimes luck was on the right side. But, the room was mostly filled with button-down shirts and a couple of construction workers. He struck up a conversation with the bartender. She called herself Jennifer, and was very friendly towards him once she saw his money clip. After a second drink he got to the point.

"Say Jennifer, I'm looking for a couple of my friends, Raul and Marcel who are visiting here from L.A." He made up the names just to make it more casual.

"We get a lot of men in here, hon, and the names don't mean much," she said, bending over the sink right in front of him and washing cocktail glasses.

Bob was focused on the problem. "They're from L.A. They're a couple of doctors, clean-cut Latino guys about thirty years old, maybe even wearing suits. I sent them here a couple of nights ago to find some escorts while they were in town," he lied, but she bought it, or she really didn't care.

"Oh yeah, I do remember the doctors. We don't get too many of those in here. Big tippers. You see that girl dancing on stage. Her name is Monica. She was hanging out with them at the table. I think she and her girlfriend left with them. Check with her."

Bob thanked her, dropped a twenty on the bar, and moved closer to the stage. When Monica finished her routine, he motioned for her to join him at a table. She nodded, picked up the dollars thrown onstage for her and exited the stage. In five minutes she came to Bob's table and sat on his lap, hoping for a table dance from him.

"Listen gorgeous, I'm looking for a couple of my friends from Los Angeles. You might know them. They were in here two nights ago. A couple of doctors."

"Oh, yes. I remember those two guys. They looked like high school teachers. Sherry and I entertained them most of the night. They were real nice guys. Didn't drink much, but got right to the point, if you know what I mean," she giggled and kissed Bob on the neck.

"So, where did they take you?"

She pulled back and looked Bob squarely in the eye. "Say, you're not a cop are you?"

"No, just trying to find my friends. I want to have a drink with them while they're here."

Bob ordered her a glass of champagne and another red wine for himself. He flipped a hundred on the waitress and Monica took notice immediately. When the waitress returned with the change, he pushed a fifty into Monica's thong. Immediately she kicked her friendliness up a notch.

"So, what's your name handsome?"

"Mark," he lied, as she pushed her ass deeper into his groin.

"Monica. My friends. Where did you go with them?" He had to remind her of their conversation, as she was more concerned with giving him his money's worth.

"Oh them. They were brothers. I think they were called Menendez or something like that. Names are not important to me. My girlfriend and I went to their room and had a party." She giggled.

Bob needed her complete attention for his next question, so he grabbed her by the hips and stopped her gyrations. He looked right at her.

"Where are they staying, maybe I can find them there?"

"Over at the Embassy Suites. Say, do you want to go out tonight after my shift? I can show you a real good time."

"Yes, I'd like that honey. What time do you get off?"

"Three tonight. Come on by then and I'll treat you real nice. I can bring my girlfriend, Sherry, if you're into that."

"Sounds good to me, I'll be here," he lied again. He had no intention of showing up. He had what he came for and now just wanted her off his lap. "Okay, I gotta go see my friends and I'll be back later, okay?"

She got the hint he wanted to leave so she got up and kissed him on the neck again and whispered into his ear, "I can do wonders with my tongue. You'll see."

Bob rushed out and headed back to Don's house. All the blinds were drawn and he passed by slowly, parked a block away and walked back to the house, surveying the street and every car on it. It seemed clear. He knocked and identified himself, Don opened the door and Bob slipped inside.

"How'd it go?" Don was anxious.

"Perfect, I think. I got some important information from the lovely Monica. Call your friend at the FBI and see if he can run a criminal check on two men, last name is Menendez. They could be brothers."

"My new friend Monica said they took her to the Embassy Suites over by ASU. I think we might be on to these assholes now."

Chapter 25
STAKEOUT

NOW THEY WERE getting somewhere. This is what both Don and Bob liked, making progress in the case, rather than sitting and waiting for something to happen. They grabbed a sandwich and sat down at the kitchen table to go over the next phase of the plan. They didn't have much to go on, but then again, they didn't need much. It didn't matter who these guys were, both Don and Bob had a pretty good idea about what was going to happen.

Just as they finished eating, Don's cell phone rang. It was the FBI.

"I ran that criminal check for you. Couldn't come up with much, but here's what I got. Eight years ago a guy named Jorge Menendez was arrested in Baton Rouge for arson of a shipping company office. He's about the same age as your guy. No sign of a brother though. He never went to trial and wasn't convicted. He had a tight alibi. That's all that came up on the radar. If that's their real name, they've been pretty quiet or they're using another name."

"Does the report state his nationality?" Don stared

over at Bob.

"Yes, he's from Venezuela. He was in Baton Rouge on a legal visa at the time."

Don's gut wrenched. There was no denying now that all of this was related to the Venezuelan mission and Kroslak. It wasn't what Don wanted to hear, but what he knew was the truth.

"No mention of a brother traveling with him?"

"No, that's all we have. Do you think this is the guy following you around Phoenix?"

"It's possible. I'll know more later. Thanks buddy. You've been a real help."

Don immediately called Detective Hennessey to prove he was serious and maybe get some help. Don laid out the whole situation and made up some bullshit about the Venezuelan connection being related to his Chicago police work.

"Don, listen to me," Hennessey began to warn him. "I know you're a retired cop but don't go out there and take the law into your own hands. If what you're saying is true, these guys are bad news and not people you want to take on by yourself. Besides, you have no authority here in Phoenix. We'll start digging and I'll beef up the patrols at your house. We'll check out the Embassy Suites too and see if we can have a word with these guys. Just keep us in the loop if something does happen. We can handle it."

"I'll keep that in mind," Don said without much conviction, signing off.

Don repeated to Bob what the FBI agent had told him. The Venezuelan connection was the linchpin. They didn't really need to know anymore. Don and Bob knew exactly what they were dealing with now and the only way out was to be prepared for the inevitable. The police had no real idea what they were up against, and while they might be of some help, both Don and Bob knew the solution was in their hands, not those of the police.

"One arrest and no convictions in eight years. Damn, these guys must be good at what they do," Don watched for Bob's response. He was pensive.

"If they are brothers," Don said, "then these two are tight and professional, and they know how to cover their tracks. It sounds like some of our operations. Get in and get out without a trace."

"What's your gut feeling of how these guys will try to get you?" Bob asked nervously.

"Could be any way, but as long as I stay put at my house they'll make a move here, possibly a home invasion. They won't want anything public. But we're not ready for that. We need more information. For now we need to take a ride over to the Embassy Suites and see if we spot their car. I want to know where they are and what they're doing."

They took Bob's rental, which was parked a few houses down the street. On their way to the hotel Bob tried to keep the situation real. It was the only way to keep focus, and hopefully get the upper hand on these guys.

"You know as well as I do Don, when the gangs or the cartels want someone dead they'll stop at nothing to get it done. If we get these guys, and that might be a big 'if', there will be others to follow."

"I didn't need to hear that shit, but yes I know how the system works."

"You're gonna need a long-term plan," Bob answered.

When they pulled through the green and yellow neon gate to the Embassy Suites, they surveyed the cars in the parking lot.

"See anything familiar?" Bob asked.

Don grabbed Bob's arm, "Stop. There's the black Buick." He pointed it out.

"So now we know for sure where they're staying. Let's hang here and we'll do a little stakeout on these assholes. Maybe they'll make a move tonight."

They parked in a shady spot. Stakeouts in the Phoenix heat could be dangerous, so they took turns going into the hotel to cool off, cell phones at the ready. Luck seemed finally to find them, and within an hour the Menendez brothers, if that's who they were, left their room, got into the Buick, and drove away. Slowly Bob followed two hundred feet behind. After a few miles they could see the Buick was headed back towards Don's neighborhood. Then, they turned onto his street.

"Think their making a move?" Bob asked.

"It's too early. Scoping out my pad most likely. Yeah, I got a feeling they'll try to hit the place late tonight. We have to be ready."

Bob swerved off their tail and down another street. He parked the car with a view of the main road and they waited for the Buick to exit the neighborhood. This was one of the advantages of a walled-in community; there was only one way out. A couple of minutes later, the

Buick pulled out. Once they were out of view, Bob and Don drove back to the neighborhood to prepare.

They parked down the street again and walked back towards the house. Don said, "I think I have a plan. We can use my neighbor's house." He pointed to the house across the street from his.

"That's the Grossman's house. They're not here much in summer. They have an RV and they travel a lot to get out of the heat. I see the camper's gone so the house must be empty."

"OK good plan. Then we'll use their place tonight and keep watch on your house," Bob was on board quickly, as usual.

"That's right. I'm sure they wouldn't mind, but they have a burglar alarm in the house so we'll set up outside, out of sight. But, we have to work fast. I have a gut feeling this could go down any time now. And if the police start talking to these guys, they'll likely push their own timetable ahead to get it done and get out of here."

They went around back and inside Don's house and began to prepare for the stakeout across the street. The house had to appear like Don had gone to bed so they turned off the lights, except for the light in the front study. In his bedroom they pulled an old trick. They stuffed pillows under the sheets and comforter in his bed to appear he was asleep. They made sure the doors were locked, exited out the back and took up their positions across the street behind a low concrete wall.

Stakeouts are a bitch. It's always a waiting game. Sometimes it works out and sometimes it's a waste of time. The hard part was you had to be ready to respond at all times. This one was no different, and by two o'clock the night air was chilling, even in Phoenix. There had been very little traffic on the street. A police cruiser passed by an hour earlier, but nothing since then. So much for the beefed up patrols Hennessey had promised.

"Well, looks like things have caught up with me," Don couldn't help but become introspective as they sat outside in the dark in his neighbor's yard, watching his own house and waiting for something horrific to happen.

"And I'm the one that got you into all this in the first place." Bob's guilt finally surfaced.

"Nah, I've never done anything I didn't want to do. The kicker though is I had decided after the last mission I was done. Venezuela was a tough one and I'd had enough. I guess I started to worry too much about Diana and the family and what might happen. And now, here it is."

"I know. This one kind of snuck up on us. I always knew something like this *could* happen, but I never thought it really would. We were always top-notch professionals, in and out. I have to wonder how smart it was to put you in country for two weeks and get so close to that priest."

"No shit. I had my doubts even at the time, but it was a good plan and we did take Kroslak out. I don't know. I couldn't have taken out the priest, but he's probably the one that nailed me. Who knows though. It could have been anyone at the party at Kroslak's that night too."

"Yeah, way too many people saw you and saw you

close up. Well, after we take care of these guys we'll have some time to think. Any ideas on what to do next?" Bob was trying to stay positive and keep Don that way too.

Don drew a deep breath. "I know we're supposed to be on our own, it was part of the deal, but this situation is extreme. You know we have some leverage here. If anyone were to find out what we've done, there'd be an uproar. Somehow Peter's got to hear about this and contact me or you to talk about what can be done. We did our part, and sure we got paid for it, but that shouldn't mean our own government should stand silent while the cartel takes out American citizens on American soil."

"I had the same feeling as I was driving back from Christie's. They've got more information on these guys than we've been able to dig up in the past twenty-four hours. They know all about them, who their bosses are, and they've got the weapons to protect us. I mean, we can probably take out these two guys with what we've got, but if we do it will only send a message that the cartel needs bigger guns or bombs or some other shit we can't handle."

Thinking of what they could handle, at least at this moment, Don clarified the plan again, "If they show up let them go in and do what they do. They'll go straight upstairs to take care of me. They'll be quick too. Remember, your job is to take out the tires on the car first. I'll get ready for them by the door when they come back out, and then you back me up. We need to try to grab them. Having them in custody might be good for us. But, if there is a shootout make damn sure you aim correctly. Shit is going to happen fast so keep a level head."

Don knew Bob had been through this plenty of times before. They both had. When the time came, thanks to all of their training and experience, they would perform and perform well.

The waiting continued another hour and then another and it looked like no one was going to show up. Just before light, they were about to call it a night when up the street they saw a car slow down and douse its headlights.

Chapter 26
TAKE DOWN

THE BLACK BUICK slowly came to a stop on the street in front of Don's house. Don and Bob readied there weapons and crouched behind the wall, ready to move. It was go time. The car pulled up right in front of Don's house. There was no doubt now. Two men jumped out of the vehicle carrying automatic pistols and rushed to the door, kicking it in.

Without a word to each other Don and Bob immediately leapt into action, and they quietly and quickly rushed across the street with guns drawn. Don parked himself by the front door, and Bob pumped two silent rounds into the tires of the black Buick. In seconds they saw flashes of light and heard a barrage of gunfire from inside the house. These guys didn't care about silencers. Suddenly, the men were yelling at each other in Spanish. Don knew exactly what was going on as he stood ready by the door. He pictured feathers flying all over his bedroom as the killers shot up his pillow instead of his body. He heard scuffling and more gunshots, some angry voices. Don was sure they were shooting at anything at all in their anger at having been outsmarted. The sound of their feet on the tile floor came closer, and the two men came running out of the doorway. Don's whole body was tensed and ready to fire. As the first Venezuelan rushed through the door, no doubt thinking he was home-free on his escape to the car, Don threw his whole body into him, knocking him backwards onto the concrete landing and right into his buddy. Don was like a raging bull, and they all landed hard. Hard enough to give Don and Bob time. One of them gathered himself and swung his weapon in Bob's direction, but Bob was already running towards him, and Bob had real good aim. Before the scumbag could fire, he took a bullet in the stomach from Bob's Glock. He hit the ground screaming and writhing in pain. Bob turned his attention to Don, but of course he didn't need any help. Don had his man pinned to the ground face down with the full force of his left knee, with his arms wrenched up tightly behind his back. Don was pissed and had the guy screaming out in pain. Another side of Don had taken over. His laser-like focus was on survival and this man stood in his way. His instinct said to kill him. His right hand, which was shoving the Beretta, locked and loaded, into the guy's skull, wanted to pull that trigger. These guys had invaded his territory, they were at his goddamn house, and Don wanted so bad to pop him right then and there. Bob's voice was the only sound that got through.

"Hold him Don. We got them. I hear sirens. Just hold him"

Don eased just a bit, feeling the flood of reality come in to his consciousness. Every muscle was in play, focused on keeping this guy right where he was, but his mind was now taking in the surroundings. Bob was standing over the other guy doubled over on the front walkway, gun pointed at his head should he make a bad decision. Bob kept talking to Don.

"Tell me if you need help with him. This guy's done for. Just hold on. They're almost here."

Don's dreamlike haze lifted. He was back in reality, "I'm good. I've got him."

"You picked the wrong guy to fuck with, eh amigo?" Don said as he jammed his knee harder into the guy's back. A big moan told Don that the popping sound he heard was the crack of a rib or two.

By now the cover was blown, and neighbors had come out of their houses to see what the commotion was all about. There was no need to ask for help, one of them had already called the police. A few long seconds later, five squad cars broke the eerie dawn silence, screaming down the quiet residential neighborhood with sirens blaring and screeching to a halt on the scene. A new round of chaos ensued as the police officers, not knowing who was who and trained not to ask, surrounded Don and Bob with guns drawn, yelling for them to freeze and put down their guns.

With the one suspect on the ground with a bullet in him and the other held down under two hundred ten pounds of Don's grip, the local police had no idea what they had walked into. Tension was high so Bob put down his gun and Don laid his next to the face of his guy, but didn't let up one bit on his hold or the knee he was shoving into the asshole's back.

The detective in charge came across the lawn taking in the whole situation. "What's going on here?"

Don spoke up, "I'm Don Ballantine and this is my house, and these two cocksuckers came in and tried to kill me, just like I told you was going to happen."

"We spoke on the phone, I'm Hennessey."

"And who is this guy?" Hennessey asked, pointing to Bob.

"A friend of mine who came here to help me apprehend these bastards."

"And these two?"

"My guess is this is Jorge Menendez and his brother. They've been following me for days and I needed to protect myself. So, Bob and I here did what we were trained to do. We staked out my own house and took care of the problem when it arrived."

Don had some trouble hiding his frustration with the local police. He knew it wasn't their fault, he's the one that brought this on, and he hadn't been able to explain it all to them. He still couldn't, at least not now. Maybe not ever.

The paramedics leapt into action and were treating the gunshot wound to the one brother. The whole scene was one big mess with all the police, and medical personnel running frantically back and forth. The Buick sagged at the curb on its flat tires, front doors open. Don's house had a gaping hole where the front door used to be and the smell of gunfire was wafting out to the front yard. The neighbors were all out of their houses standing around the edge of the scene, huddled together in small groups, certainly wondering what was going on with Don. He was sure he'd have to do some explaining later. He already knew his lines though. Detectives were sealing off the house and checking out the damage inside. Don released the other brother. He didn't put up any more of fight. The cracked ribs must have slowed him down some and he was handcuffed and put in the squad car.

The sun was coming up on a brand new day.

"So Don, I'm glad it worked out, but this was a pretty stupid move. You should have done what I told you and called me," said Hennessey.

"There was no time for that. I'd be dead now if I had." Don did his best to choke back his anger and distaste.

"Well, it's no wonder both of you weren't killed. Why did these guys have it in for you anyway?"

"I have no idea. I probably sent their father to jail in Chicago or something like that."

"Well, we'll find out. We'll get to the bottom of it for you. At least you're safe now." Hennessey had no idea how he sounded.

Don and Bob shared a look. They were both thinking the same thing. It was not likely that Detective Hennessey from the Mesa Police Department would ever get to the bottom of this one. And Don had no intention of helping him out. Neither one knew what was next, but they both knew that bringing Hennessey in on it now would do no one any good. It was best to wait for Peter to contact one of them.

Suddenly there was calm. The quiet had set in. The quiet that happens after a traumatic event, after all the commotion. Don and Bob slowly walked into the house, neither satisfied nor relieved by the events of the past few days. Don would have to call Diana and let her know it was safe to return—for now. Then he'd have to figure out how to break it to her that the house was shot up. She wasn't going to like this one.

Don's heart was heavy. After all, Diana was the love of his life. He would do anything to keep this marriage together and not lose her. The realization hit him hard. He needed help. His PTSD had taken his other marriages, and if he didn't get himself some treatment at the V.A. right away, he risked losing the best thing that had ever happened to him. Diana was his life and his breath now, and he couldn't bear the thought that his problems could end it all. Enough was enough. They would work together after this, and he would make sure that their life was safe, fun, and full of love for a long time to come.

Bob would go back to Los Angeles.

Don would once again be alone with his thoughts, trying to stay afloat as the waves of flashbacks and the panic of possible future attacks rode over him. Maybe it was time to head to the V.A. to handle what was clearly PTSD, because he knew now he would do whatever he could to hold his marriage together. After all, Diana was his life and his breath. But, he also knew his choices had tied him to this life for as long as he drew a breath. Don may have decided to give up the life, but it was clear now that there was no way out.

Three Men, Three Outside Contractors

Don Ballantine

Don was the senior of this small group of outside contractors. He grew up on the mean streets of Chicago. At fourteen he was a member of a gang that stole cars. He was arrested, but as a juvenile he was sentenced to probation and the watchful eyes of his Mother. His life changed at seventeen when his Mother signed the paperwork for him to join the U.S. Army, before his eighteenth birthday, while the Vietnam War was in full swing. He married his sweetheart, Linda, and soon after shipped out to Vietnam. In "Nam" he became a man, fighting in the jungles and facing death on every patrol. He gained the respect of his buddies for his courageous fighting ability in the face of the enemy. He was assigned to the prestigious First Calvary Division and wore their patch proudly. Nearing New Year's Eve in his seventh month, he was injured while in a firefight with the North Vietnamese Army. His unit, showed intense bravery while enduring three straight days of combat, during which they were able to destroy the Six Ten Yellow Shining Star Division of North Vietnam. For his unit's conduct under fire, the entire unit was awarded the Presidential Unit Citation by President Lyndon Baines Johnson. Don personally was awarded a Vietnamese Gallantry Cross and a Purple Heart.

From his exposure to continuous battle, Don suffered from what is now known as post-traumatic stress disorder. This would eventually lead to the destruction of his first marriage and caused extreme stress on his children, which he regretted his whole life.

Bob Kiser

Bob Kiser was a ten-year veteran of the Marine Corp. He trained in Camp Lejeune, North Carolina and volunteered for duty in Iraq and Afghanistan. His specialty was mine-sweeping and removal of explosive devices. After three tours of duty in the Middle East he was assigned to a detachment of military police in Leavenworth, Kansas. After his service, he became more interested in law enforcement and became a member of the Georgia Bureau of Investigation. Bob was 6'2", weighed two hundred pounds and was very athletic. He kept his buzz cut from the Marines and was an imposing figure both in and out of uniform. He was capable of taking charge of any situation in the line of duty. After his retirement, and due to his exceptional record, he was hired by the State Department as an outside contractor. This led to his meeting and teaming up with his two partners, Don Ballantine and Manny Perez.

Manny Perez

Manny's parents immigrated to Miami from Cuba during the exodus of thousands of Cubans under Fidel Castro's rule. He was born and raised in a Hispanic neighborhood in South Miami. He graduated from the University of Miami with honors, majoring in law enforcement. Upon graduation, he was hired by the Miami Police Department and served as a detective. On the force, he dealt with drug trafficking, illegal immigrants, and gangs of criminals operating in Dade County. He was able to infiltrate the gangs and made numerous arrests. At times he was asked to work with the U.S. Coast Guard in stopping the massive flow of drugs arriving by boat into Dade County during the 1980's. At 42, he took training at the FBI National Academy in Quantico Virginia where he met Don Ballantine and Bob Kiser.